EXODUS
Esther Shakine

EXODUS

Esther Shakine

Graphic Novel

HIRMER

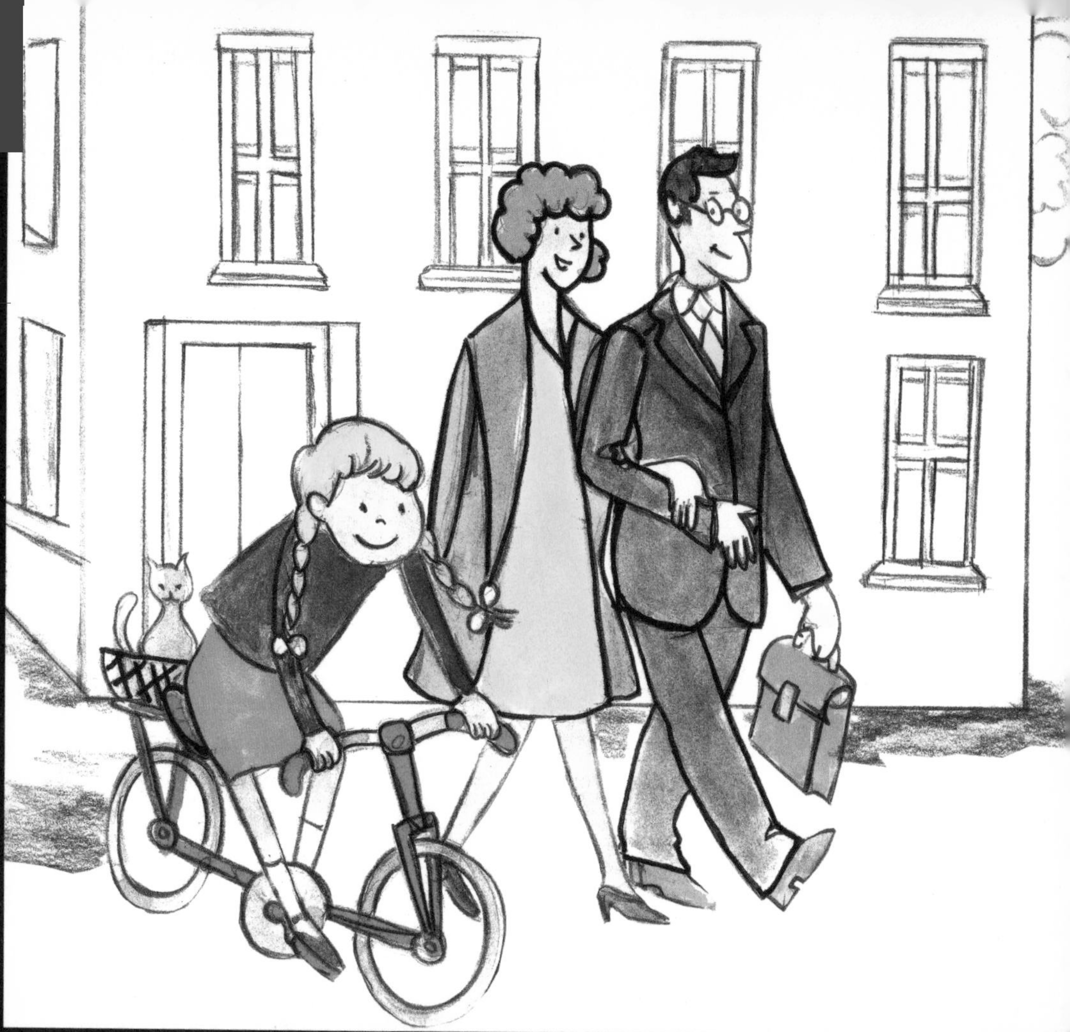

My name is Ticka.
Mummy, Daddy and I lived in a big city in southern Hungary. We had a flat with lots o
rooms that was right next to the museum and the big church. I had my own room, too.
Daddy was an engineer. He gave me a red bicycle which I wasn't allowed to ride in the flat
My parents' friends used to come round to us on Jewish holidays. I had to sing or recite
poems and everyone said: "What a lovely little girl!" I didn't like that at all. Actually, I really
wanted to be a boy and play football.
For my fifth birthday I asked for a dog but was given a cat instead. I called it Pitsy.

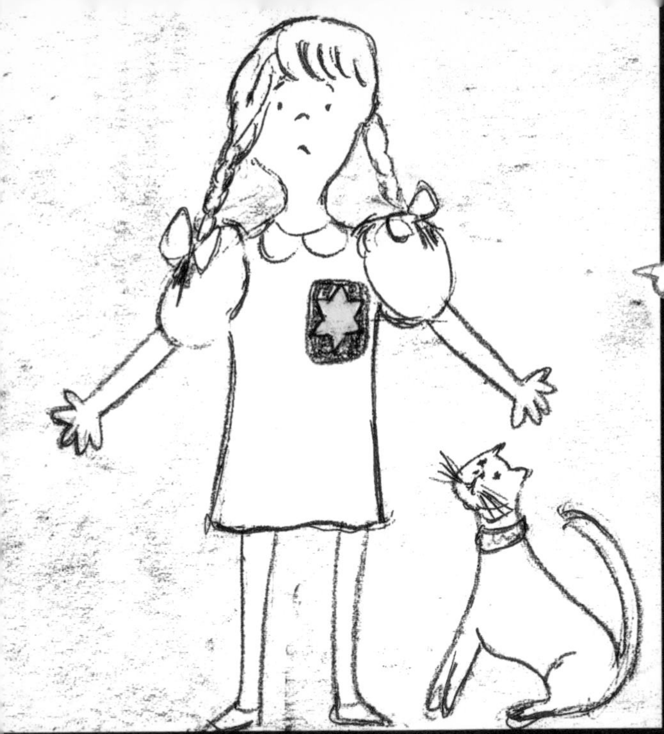

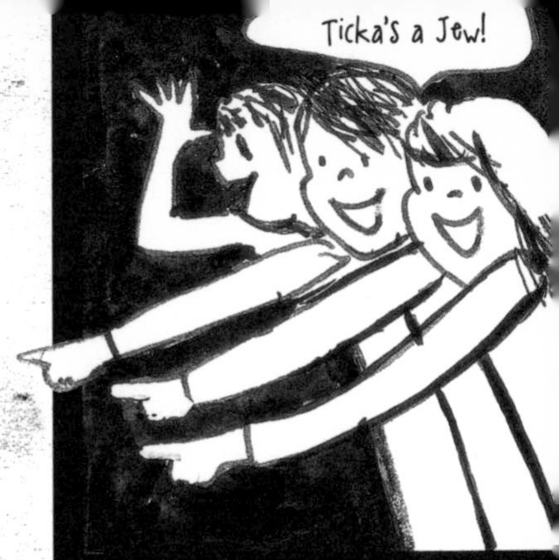
Ticka's a Jew!

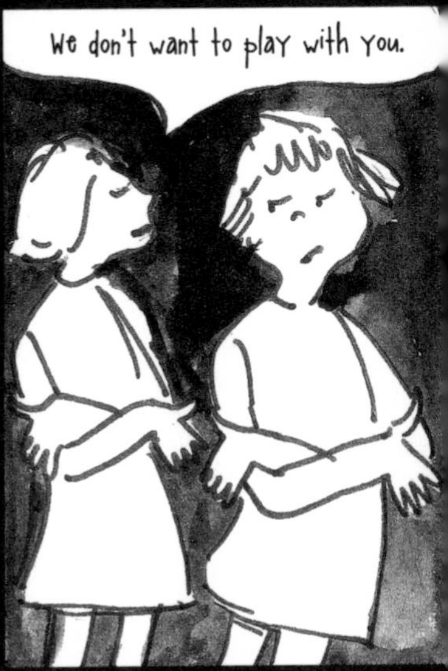
We don't want to play with you.

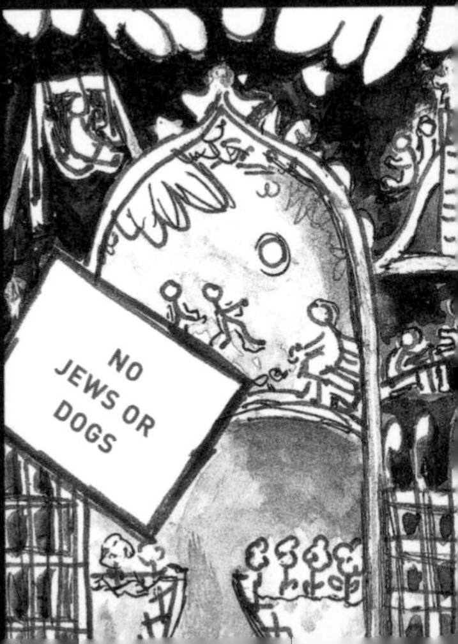
NO
JEWS OR
DOGS

One day my Mummy sewed a yellow star on my dress.
I asked her: “Why are you doing that?”
“Because we’re Jews”, she answered.
“I don’t want to wear that. It’s ugly! My friends don’t have one and nor does Pitsy!”
At first she didn’t say a word. Then she said: “You’re a big girl now, aren’t you? Listen to me carefully. There are some nasty people out there – they’re called Nazis and now they’re in charge in the city. They’ve told us we have to wear this star. We’re not allowed to take it off. Now stop crying!”
That made me cry all the more.

Open the door, you filthy Jew!
Don't say anything, Ticka!

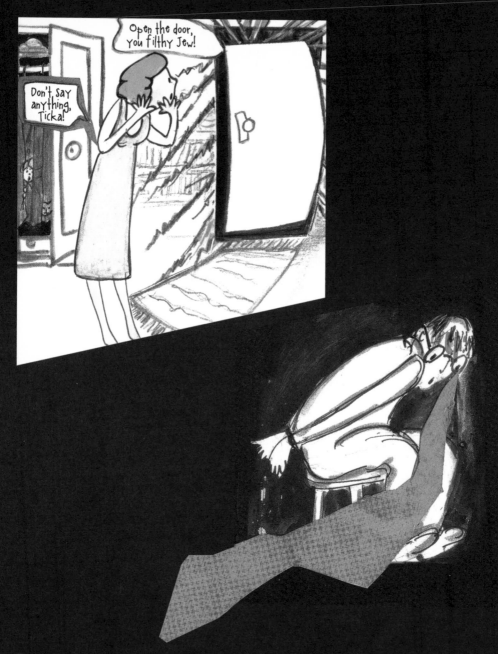

One night someone hammered on our door with his fists and kicked it. A voice called out: "Open the door, you Jews!" Mummy got me out of bed and pushed me into the cupboard between the clothes and the boxes. I wanted to scream but she said: "Keep very quiet, no matter what happens. Keep quiet! Not a word! And don't come out of the cupboard whatever you do." I scooped up Pitsy in my arms and cuddled her tightly. I could hear shouting and the sound of someone being punched. The policemen burst in with their guns in their hands. Mummy just managed to close the cupboard in time. One of the policemen looked at my bed and asked: "Where's the girl?" "She's sleeping over at her aunt's", my mother answered. That was a big fat lie as my auntie had gone to live in America. The policemen pushed Mummy to one side. Daddy was bleeding.

pressed myself up against the very back of the cupboard and cried quietly. But someone heard me: "What's that?" the policeman shouted and tore open the cupboard door. He rummaged through the clothes and some boxes fell out on the floor.

His boots were right in front of my eyes. Pitsy hissed out of fear and then shot out. The policeman tried to kick her and almost fell over as a result. "Bloody cat!" he swore. The others laughed and pushed Mummy and Daddy out of the flat. I was left on my own in the cupboard. I didn't cry any more.

I didn't cry for a long time after that either.

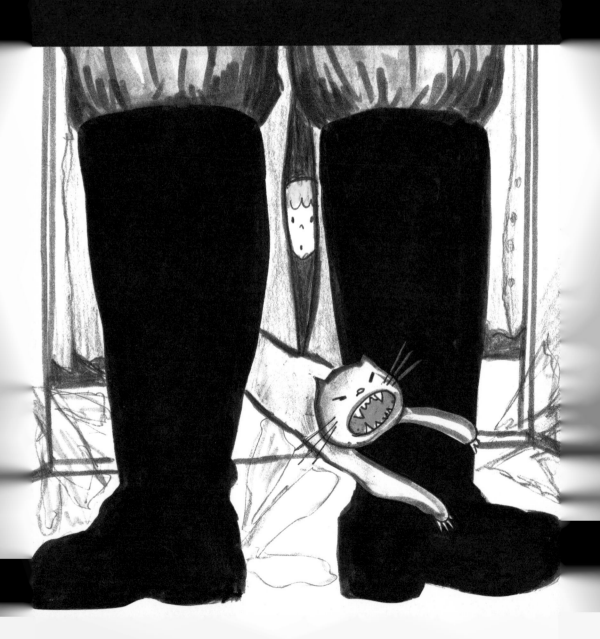

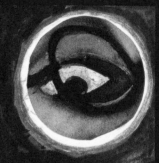

I sat in the dark for ages. When I finally dared to come out I found everything had been smashed to pieces. The neighbour didn't answer the door but I knew he had seen me through the spyhole.

Out on the street everything was quiet. Nobody took any notice of me. Then I saw a policeman and ran off towards the church. I almost bumped into a priest I knew. He always used to come to our home to play chess. He grabbed me by the arm: "What are you doing here?" "I'm looking for Mummy and Daddy", I answered. He looked quickly to the left and right and then said: "Come with me". In the church everything was absolutely silent; candles were burning and it smelt strange. Then he said: "Now let's take this star off, first of all, and forget that you ever had it". He hung a cross around my neck: "From now on you are a little Christian girl". Then he took me to the orphanage run by the convent.

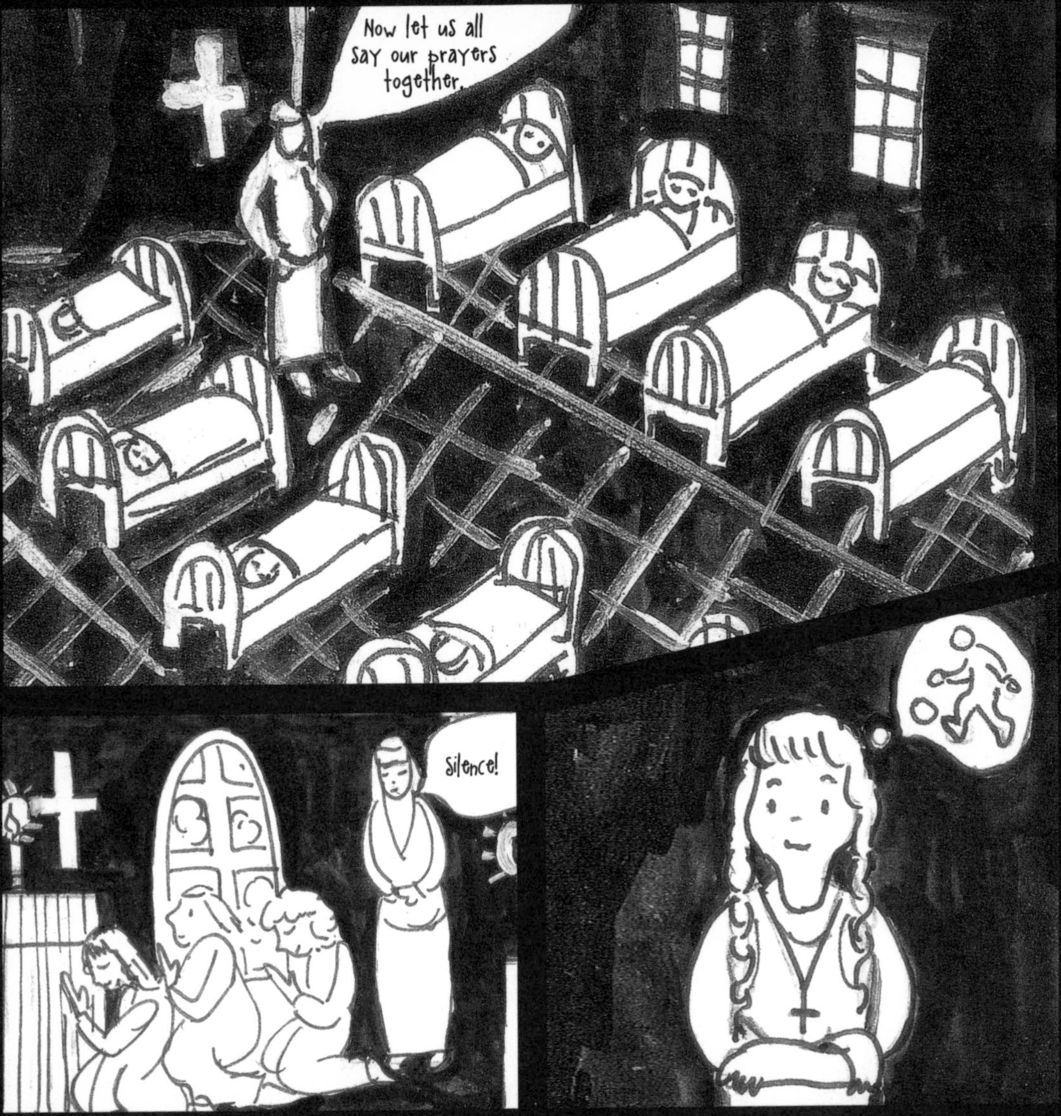
Now let us all say our prayers together.
Silence!

There were lots of girls in the orphanage. We slept in dormitories where it was very cold in winter. When we went for walks I didn't stand out at all. With my fair hair and plaits, my blue eyes and the big cross on my chest I looked just like all the others. We prayed hard but I didn't want to be a nun. I would rather have played football like my Daddy. Time passed. The war had been going on now for three years. In Germany the Nazis still did whatever their 'Führer' said. He was a horrible and brutal man. His name was Hitler. He wanted to take over the whole world with his army and he hated Jews more than anything.

He had them herded together in their thousands in districts of a town that were then called 'ghettos'. These were hidden behind high walls and there was hardly any water and not much to eat. Many people died. Those who survived were jammed into cattle wagons and taken off to camps where they were tortured and murdered.

I didn't know any of this in the convent. The only thing I knew was that it was dangerous to be a Jew.

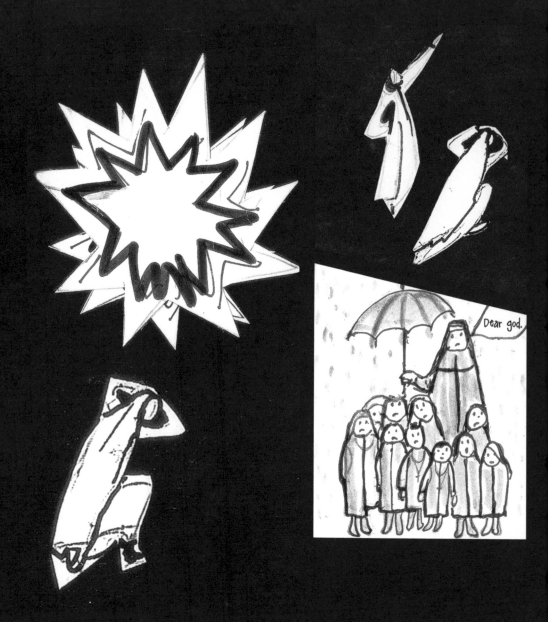

In spring the air raids started. Everybody screamed: "Oh, god, oh, god!" Each time the siren went off we had to go down into the big cellar under the church. It was full of people with lamps and candles. You could hear the planes coming and then the sound of bombs exploding. People said: "They're firing at our soldiers" and the nuns replied: "Let us pray for them". I didn't pray because, for me, soldiers were the same as policemen and they had taken my Mummy and Daddy away from me.

The bombing got closer and closer; the ground shook. Some children screamed with fear. When we came out of the cellar we could see that the houses round about were all in ruins.

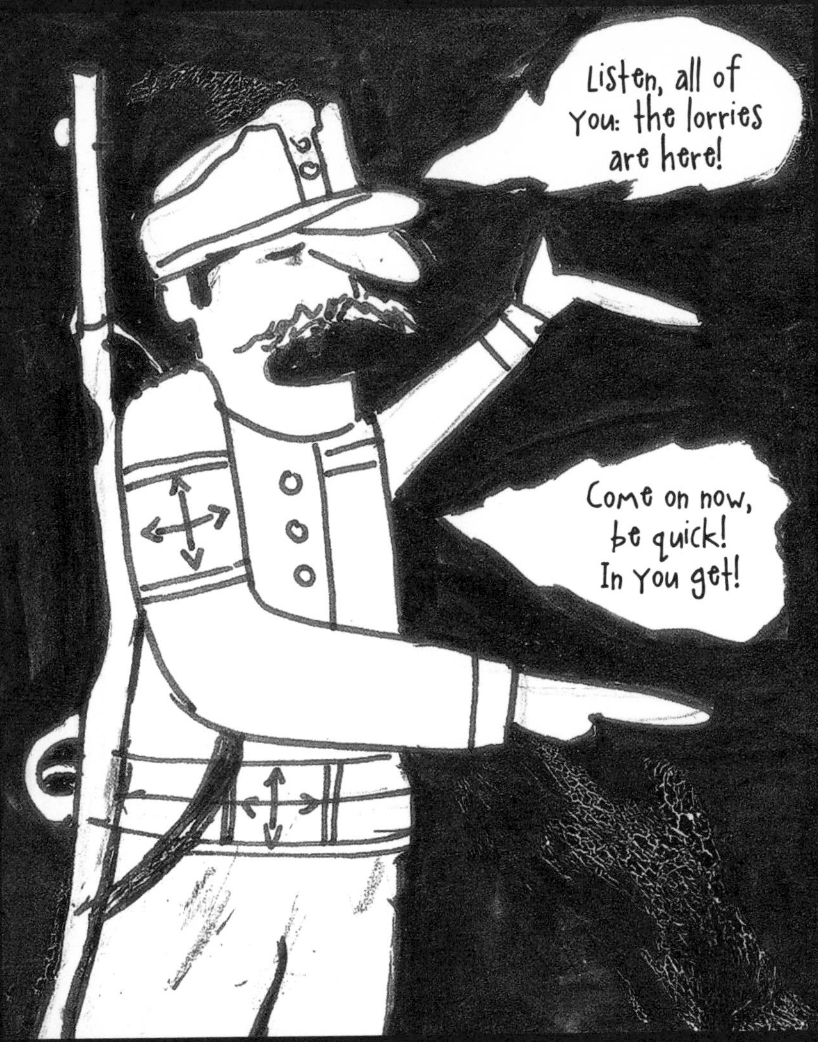
Listen, all of You: the lorries are here!
Come on now, be quick! In You get!

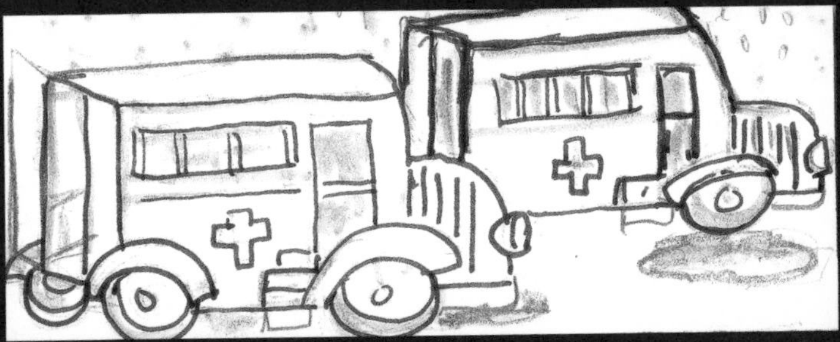

One day some lorries turned up to take us into the country. A policeman was there, too. With those same black boots again!

Those horrible boots!
Hurry up! Quick! Run!

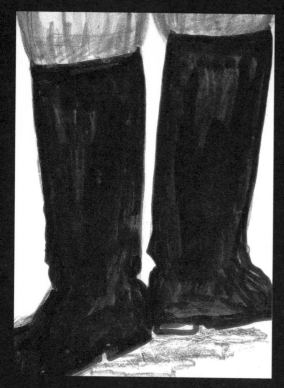

I ran off straight away – so fast that I couldn't catch my breath and got a stitch. But the only thing I wanted was to get away. Apart from me there was no one else on the road.

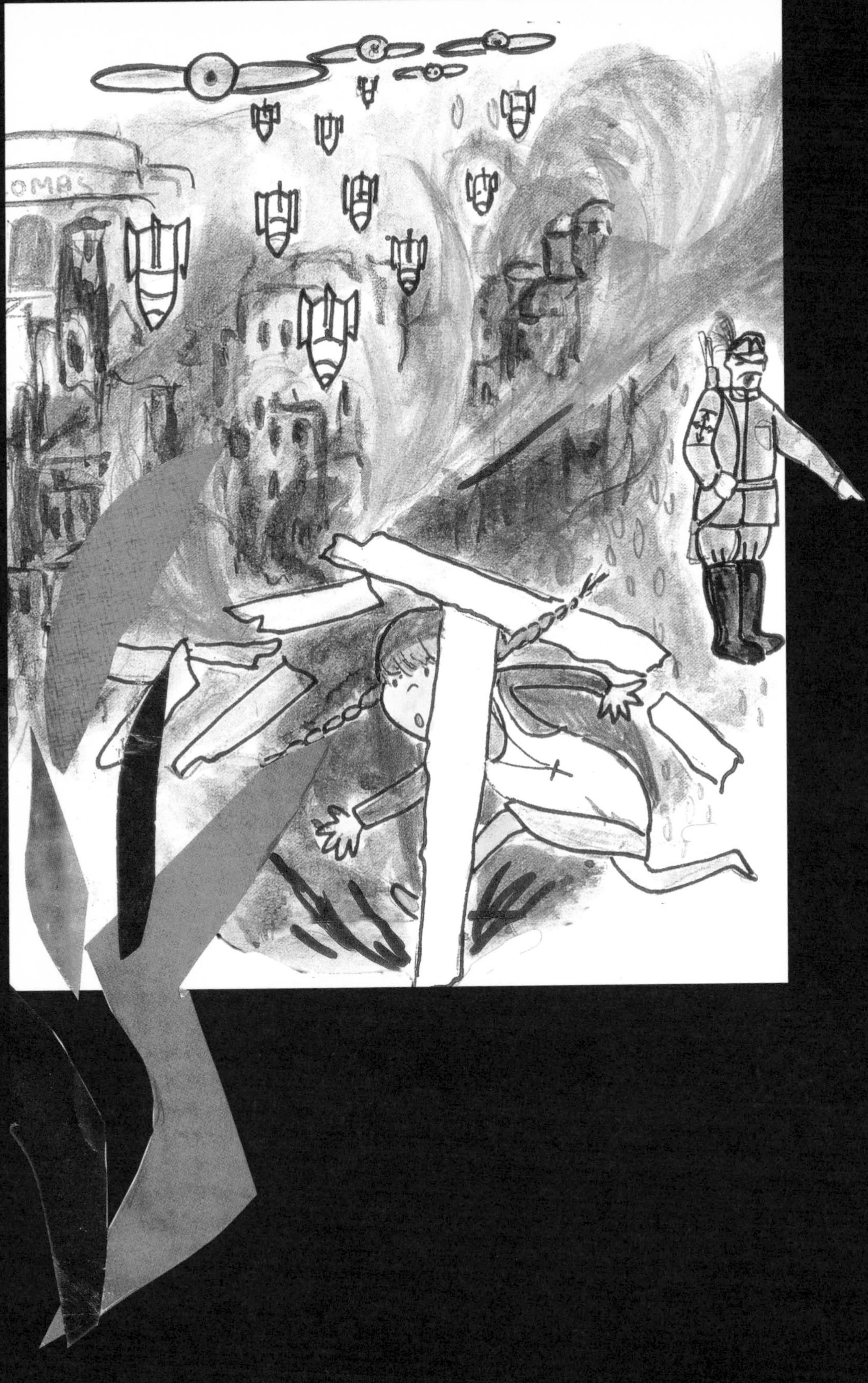

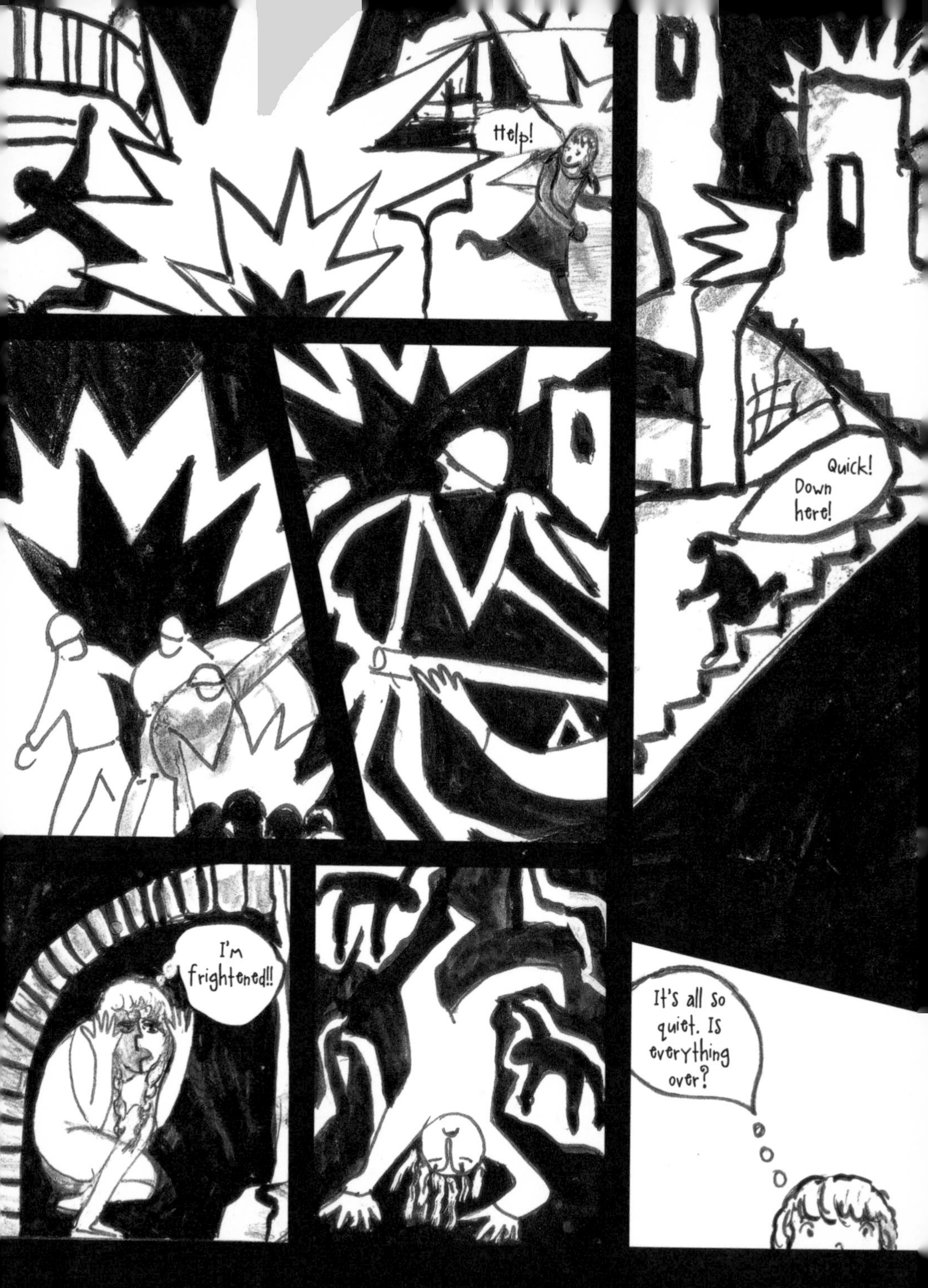
Help!
Quick! Down here!
I'm frightened!!
It's all so quiet. Is everything over?

t was horrible. I spent the whole night hiding under the stairs in a house that had been bombed and didn't sleep a wink. The next morning people were still shooting in the streets. At last everything was quiet again. I thought: "Has everything stopped? Perhaps the war is over."

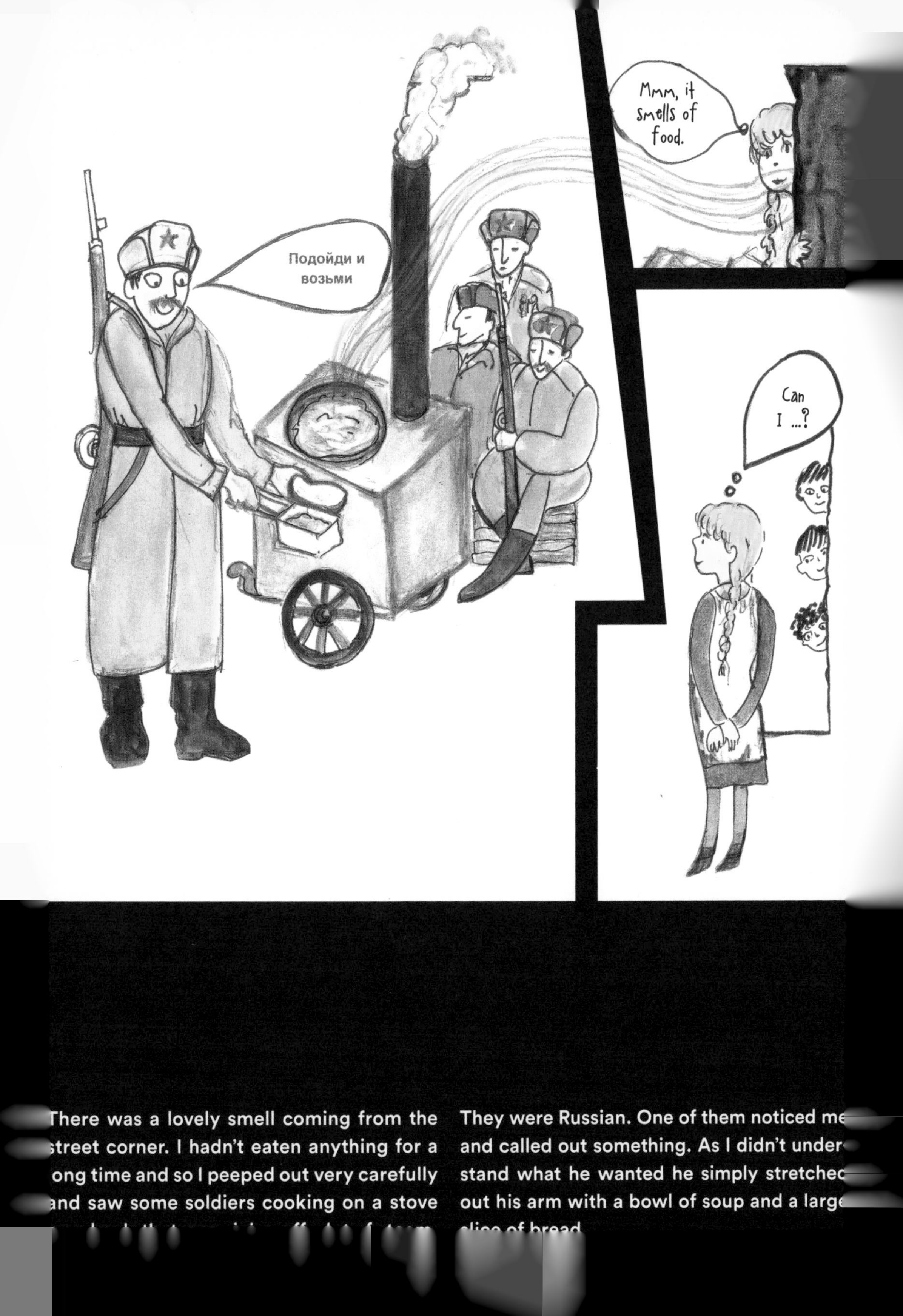
Подойди и
возьми
Mmm, it smells of food.
Can I ...?

There was a lovely smell coming from the street corner. I hadn't eaten anything for a long time and so I peeped out very carefully and saw some soldiers cooking on a stove [illegible]

They were Russian. One of them noticed me and called out something. As I didn't understand what he wanted he simply stretched out his arm with a bowl of soup and a large slice of bread.

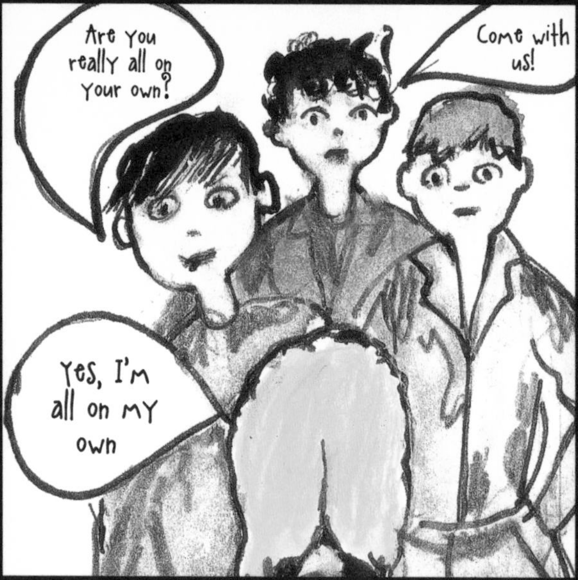
Are you really all on your own?
Come with us!
Yes, I'm all on my own

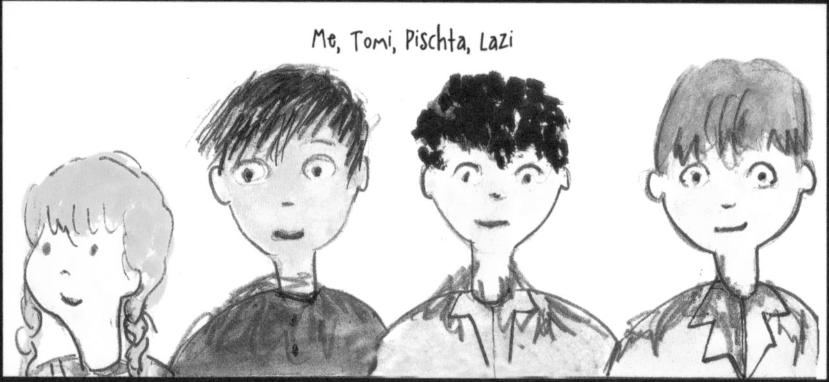
Me, Tomi, Pischta, Lazi

The smell of food had attracted three other children, too, who – like me – had been wandering around the ruins. I didn't know who they were, but I didn't want to ask any questions. They were bigger than me and scared me a bit. Then I thought: "If they have to hide then they're probably in the same position as me". That was in fact the case and each of them had a story of their own that they told me later.

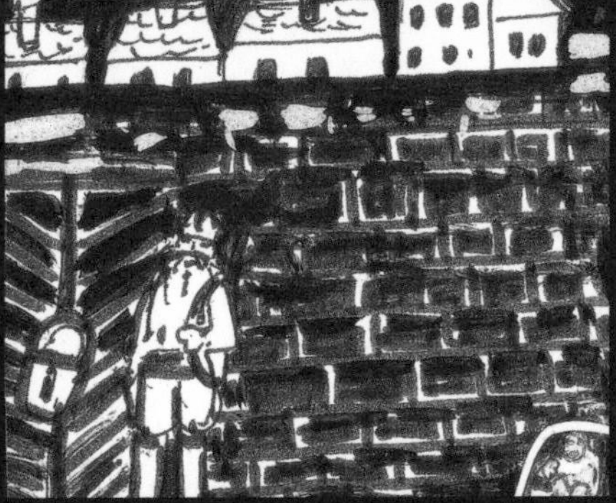

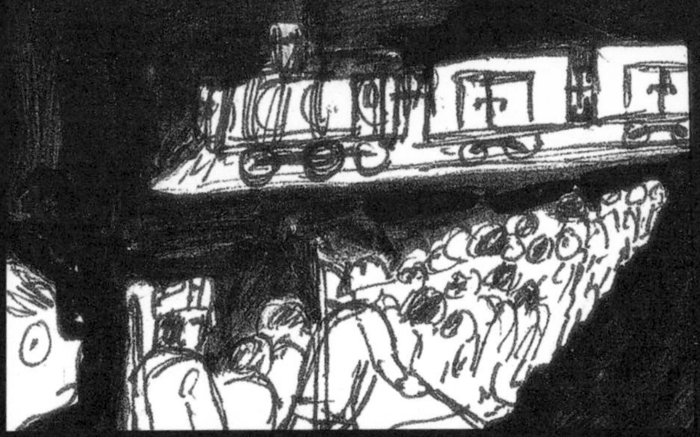

Lazi told us that there was nothing to eat in the ghetto. However, he had managed to escape through a hole in the wall and find something for his family to eat. One day, when he returned, he saw how some soldiers had come to pick up a lot of the Jews.
His parents were among them – but they pretended not to see him. He was left on his own.

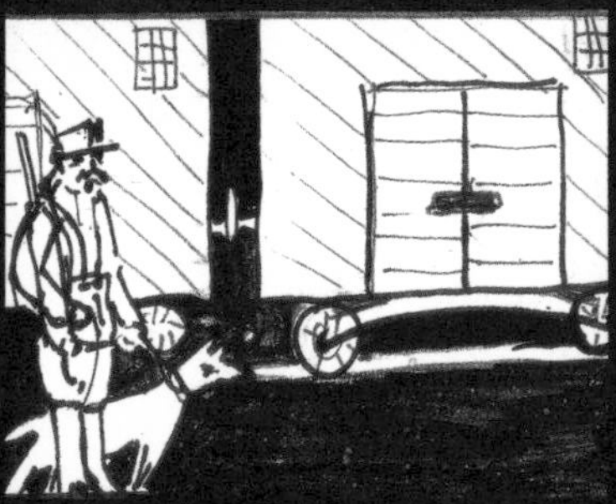

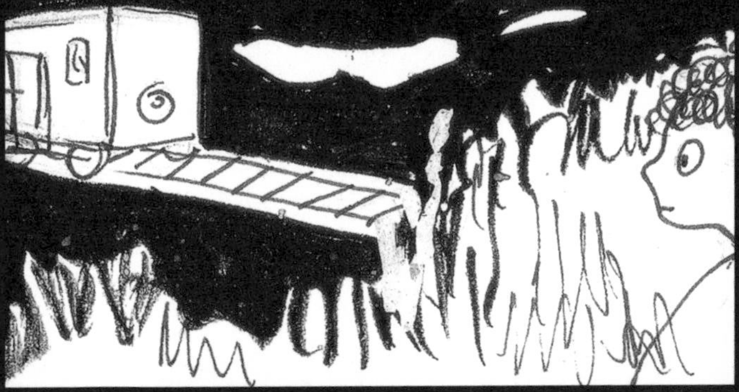

In Pischta's case the Nazis had herded all the Jews from his village into cattle wagons but he managed to jump out of the train.

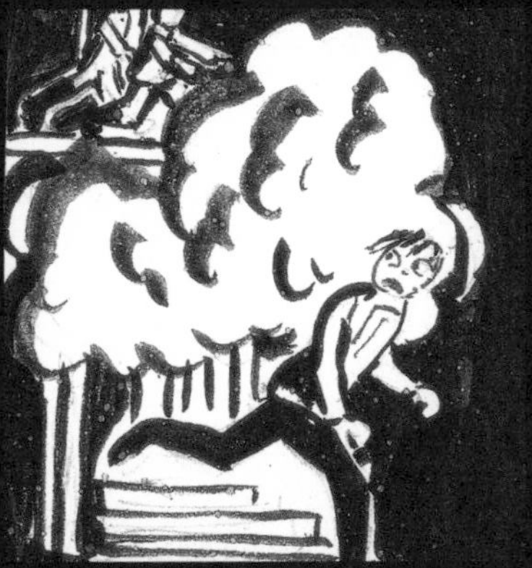

And Tomi had been able to escape from the soldiers as well.

Then we found a car and decided to make it our home. The rest of the time we carried on wandering around the ruins. Fortunately the soldiers gave us something to eat three times a day. And we even learnt a bit of Rus-

…azi, Pischta, Tomi and I – we became a proper gang of friends and stuck together

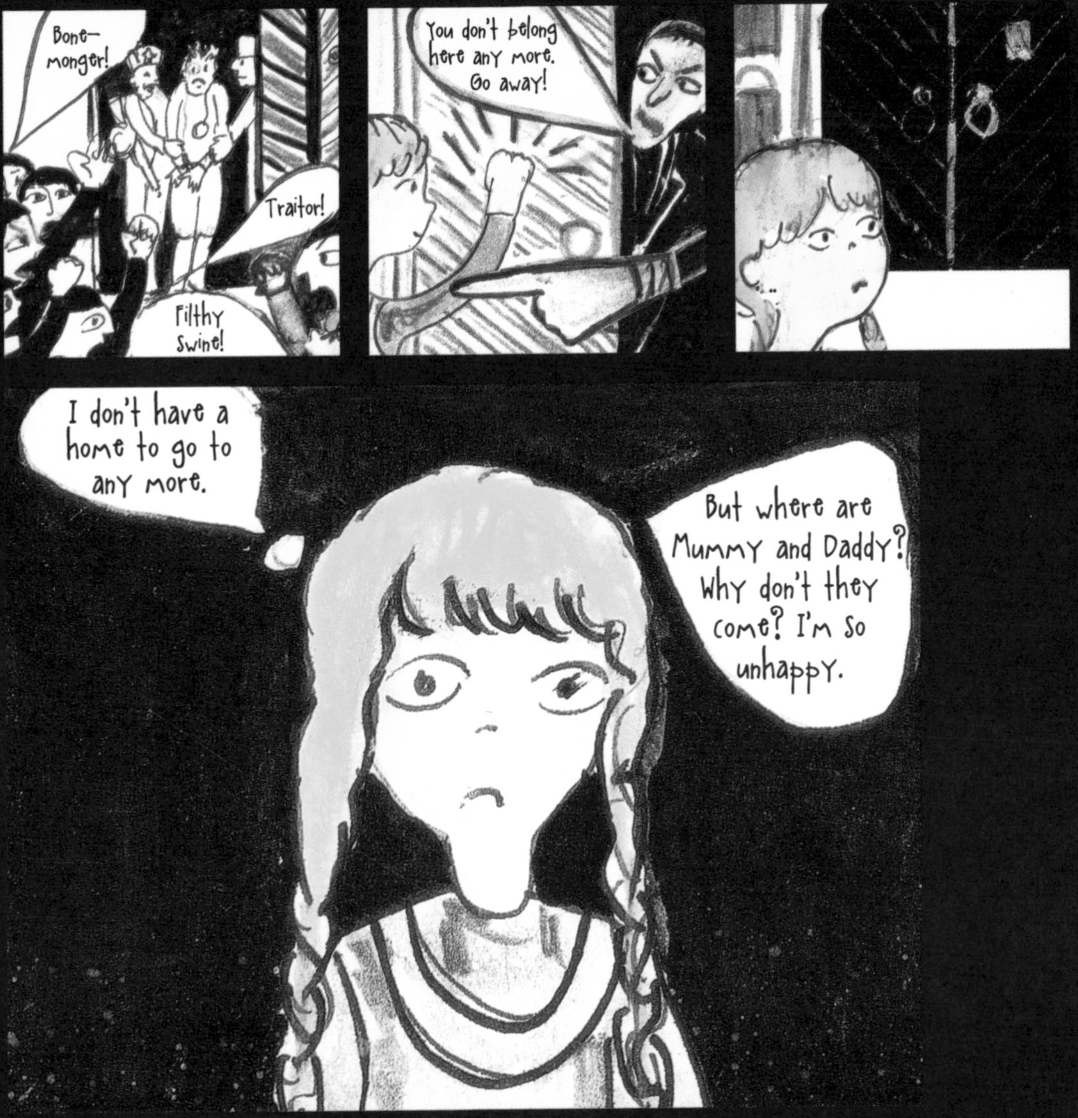
Bone-monger!
Traitor!
Filthy Swine!
You don't belong here any more. Go away!
I don't have a home to go to any more.
But where are Mummy and Daddy? Why don't they come? I'm so unhappy.

After a little while I wanted to see if Mummy and Daddy had come home again and were looking for me. When I got to our house our neighbour was being led away. He was in handcuffs. The crowd was chanting: "Filthy swine, traitor, bonemonger!"
I asked him: "Where are my parents?" But he didn't answer.

I wanted to go inside and knocked on the door. Some people were living there who I didn't know and they called out: "This is our house now. You don't belong here any more. Go away!" and slammed the door in my face.
I went back every day to look for my parents. But the door always remained firmly shut.

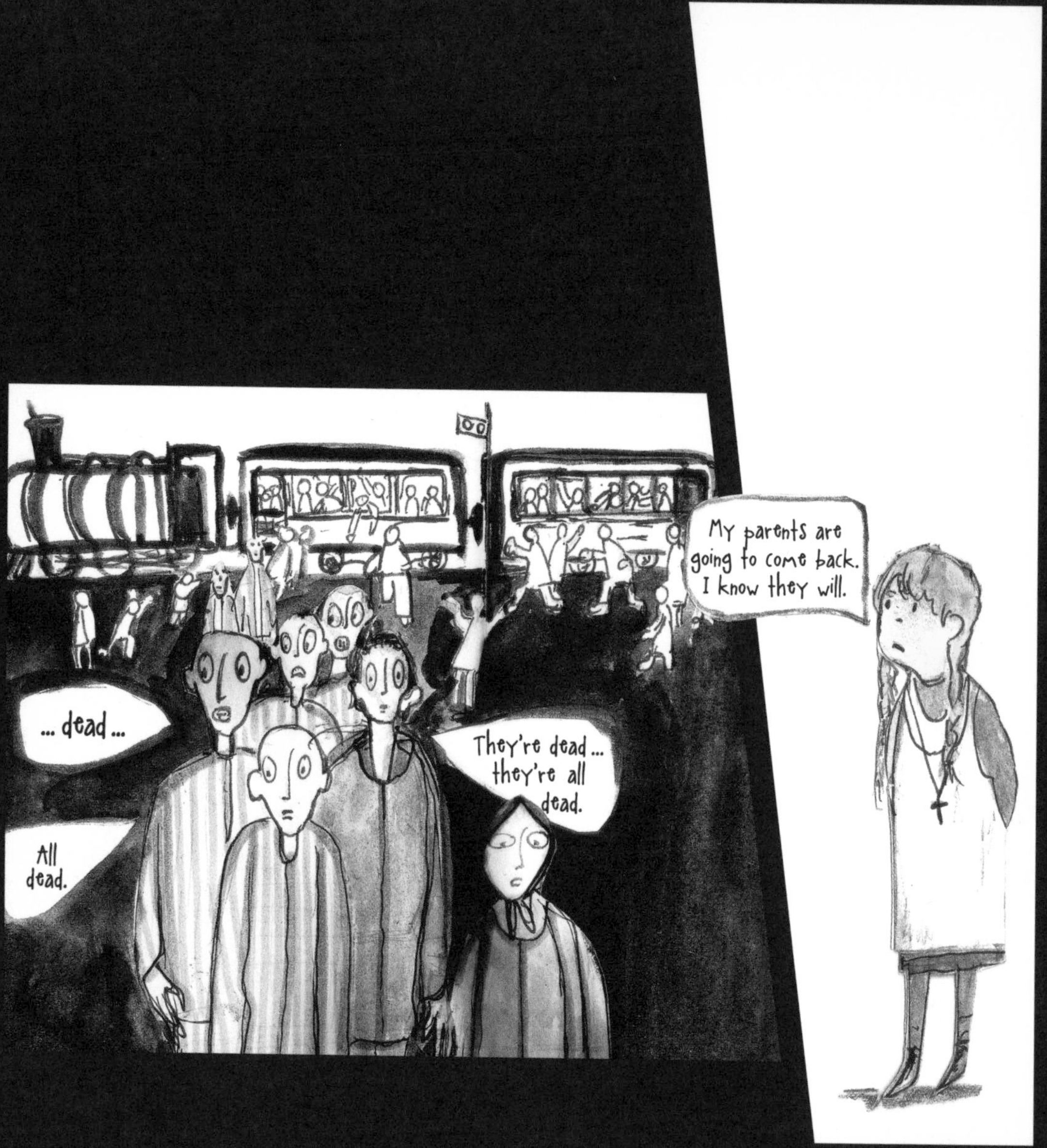
... dead ...
They're dead... they're all dead.
All dead.
My parents are going to come back. I know they will.

We guessed that our parents had been taken to a camp. We also knew in the meantime that these camps were called 'KZ' – that is short for *Konzentrationslager*, which means 'concentration camp'. Then we heard that people would soon be coming back from them. We went to the station straight away where lots of others were already waiting. Whenever a train arrived we ran up and down calling out our parents' names.

The new arrivals got out in little groups; they were wearing striped shirts or clothes which were much too big that the soldiers had given them. They were just skin and bone and when we first saw them we thought they were ghosts. We asked them questions. They simply murmured: "They're dead, they're all dead". But we didn't want to believe them and were afraid to miss the arrival of our own relatives.

Where are you from? Who are you waiting for?
חי״ל
JEWISH BRIGADE GROUP
I'm called Dan.
Who made you wear the yellow badge?
Nobody.

A soldier at the station had a yellow star on his sleeve. He spoke to me: "Are there many others waiting like you?" I ran off and came back with my friends. Tomi asked him: "Who told you to wear the yellow badge?" "Nobody", he answered with a smile. "It's my guiding star and I'm proud of it. It's a good star. A bright star."
His name was Dan. He gave us some chocolate and then told us about the Promised Land, the country of the Jews. We didn't know if we should believe him or not.
Dan suggested we go with him to a home where Jewish children without parents lived. (I wondered how he knew that I was a Jew. After all, I was still wearing my cross.) We told him that we were waiting for our parents who would soon be coming home. "Exactly", said Dan. "And where are they going to find you again?"
He took us to a big, white house. There were lots of children playing football. We were given something to eat and were shown to our rooms where there were beds with linen sheets. We were sent off to wash.
In the evening I couldn't sleep. The bed reminded me of home. I didn't know whether I should stay there or go to the station to wait for my parents.
In the morning we had breakfast in a large dining room. Then we were split into groups according to our age, which meant that I couldn't be with the others because they were older than me. "Just say that you're older", Tomi suggested. And so I managed to stay together with my friends.

My name is Atsi and I'm your group leader. I was in the resistance in the war.

My group has to be the very best. Let's see what you can all do!

I can already read and write. I learnt that in the convent.

Dan introduced a boy to us who must have been about sixteen years old. "This is Atsi your group leader." Atsi wanted us to be the best group. He started straight away with a training run and we kept up close behind him so he could see how good we were. Then we had something to eat followed by a medical check-up and then lessons.

That's our soup!

I need my knife to defend myself.

If he has to go then we go, too.

One day a group of boys from another orphanage came over. They simply grabbed all our soup and laughed at us. Tomi tipped a full bowl of soup over the ringleader's head. This led to a punch-up and the visitors then set on us with forks. Tomi pulled out his knife.

Then the group leaders turned up. Atsi called out: "Give me the knife!" "No", Tomi retorted. That was silly because they nearly threw him out. We stood by Tomi and would have gone with him, even if that had meant going back to living on the streets and back to the cold. But then Dan stepped in

In winter it got very cold. We went looking for wood among the bombed houses so that we could make a fire. Then at least we were able to keep warm from time to time.

It was early spring when our group leaders announced: "Tomorrow we're off to Israel!" There was a lot of excitement. Atsi had to quieten everyone down before he explained in a whisper: "The Hungarian government has refused to give us permission to leave the country. So we we have to pretend we are deaf-mute children from Italy so that we can cross the border. If someone asks you something, just don't answer. Is that clear?" The following day some lorries came

It was a grey and cold morning. We were driven through the city and passed close by my house. It was a strange feeling seeing it for the last time. But I was thinking mainly about the journey ahead.

Altogether we were almost 200 children at the station. Policemen were standing along the platform. Curious strangers asked us questions but nobody opened their mouths. At long last the train pulled out. In the evening we reached Austria. Some children were frightened to see

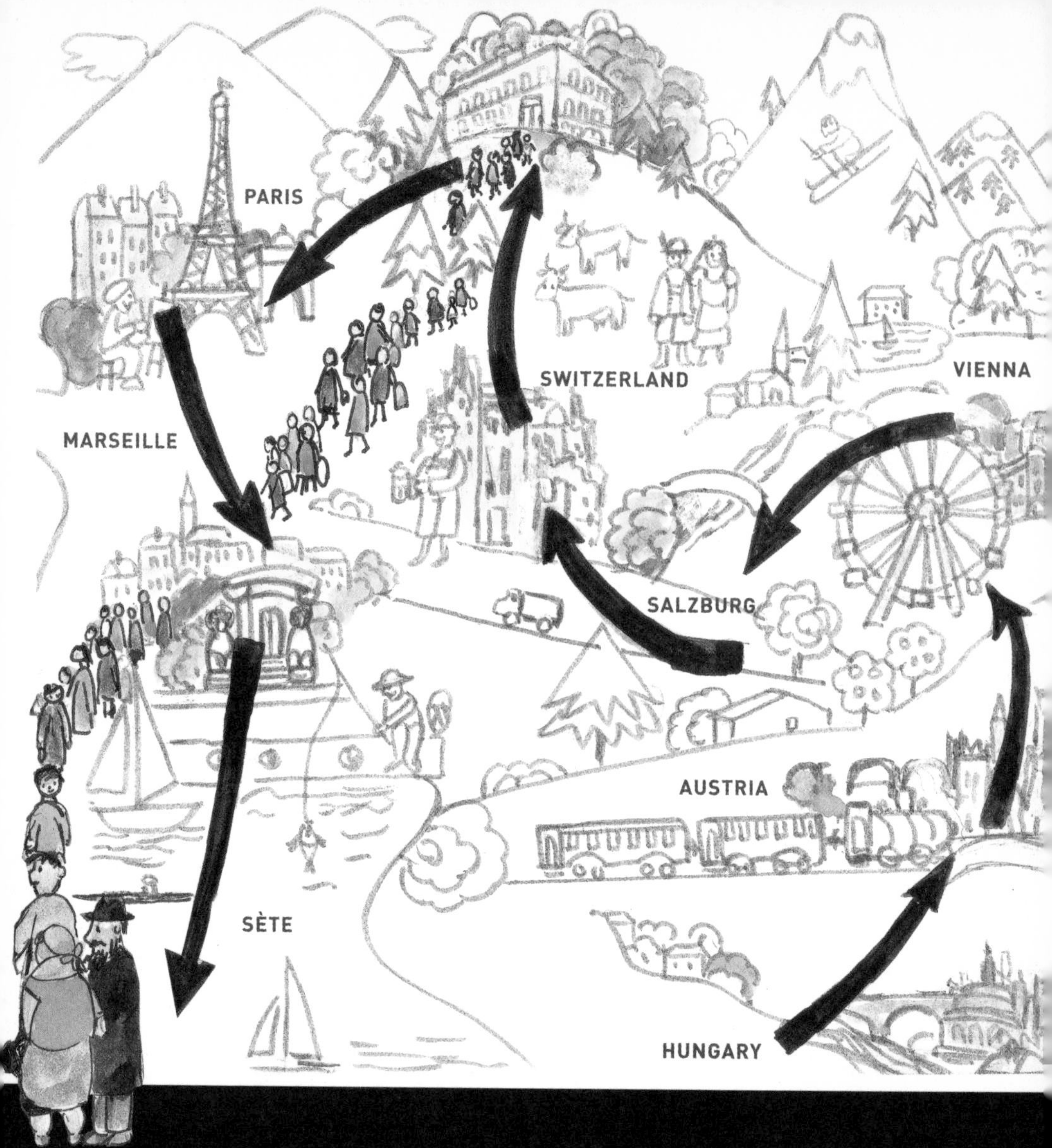
PARIS
SWITZERLAND
VIENNA
MARSEILLE
SALZBURG
AUSTRIA
SÈTE
HUNGARY

We thought the trip to Israel would take ust two or three days. We were very much mistaken as it would turn out to be an ex-

that was called Palestine in those days was ruled by Great Britain at that time and the British did not want to let Jews into their 'Eretz Yisrael' – the 'Land of Israel' – as they

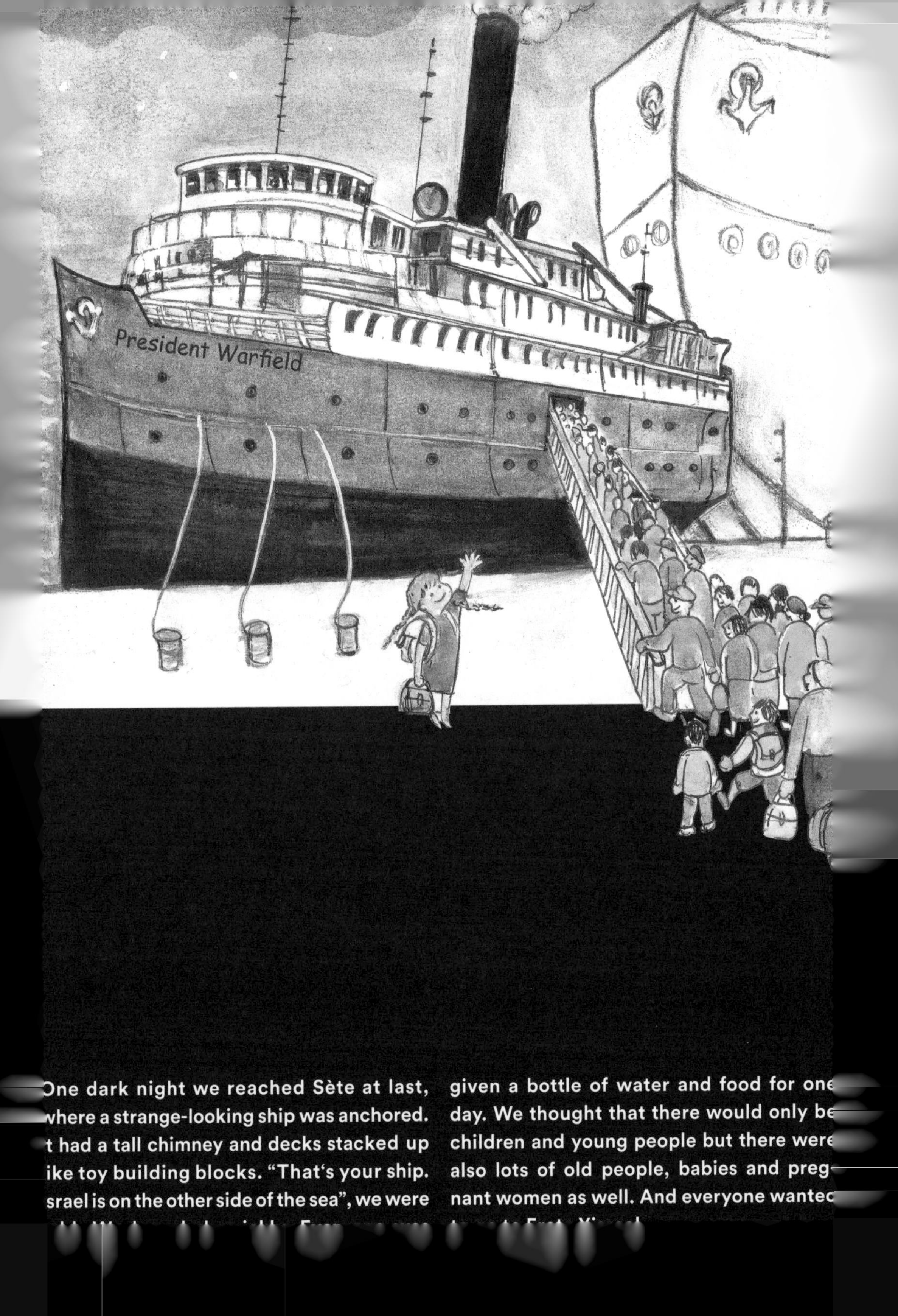
President Warfield

One dark night we reached Sète at last, where a strange-looking ship was anchored. It had a tall chimney and decks stacked up like toy building blocks. “That‘s your ship. Israel is on the other side of the sea”, we were

given a bottle of water and food for one day. We thought that there would only be children and young people but there were also lots of old people, babies and pregnant women as well. And everyone wanted

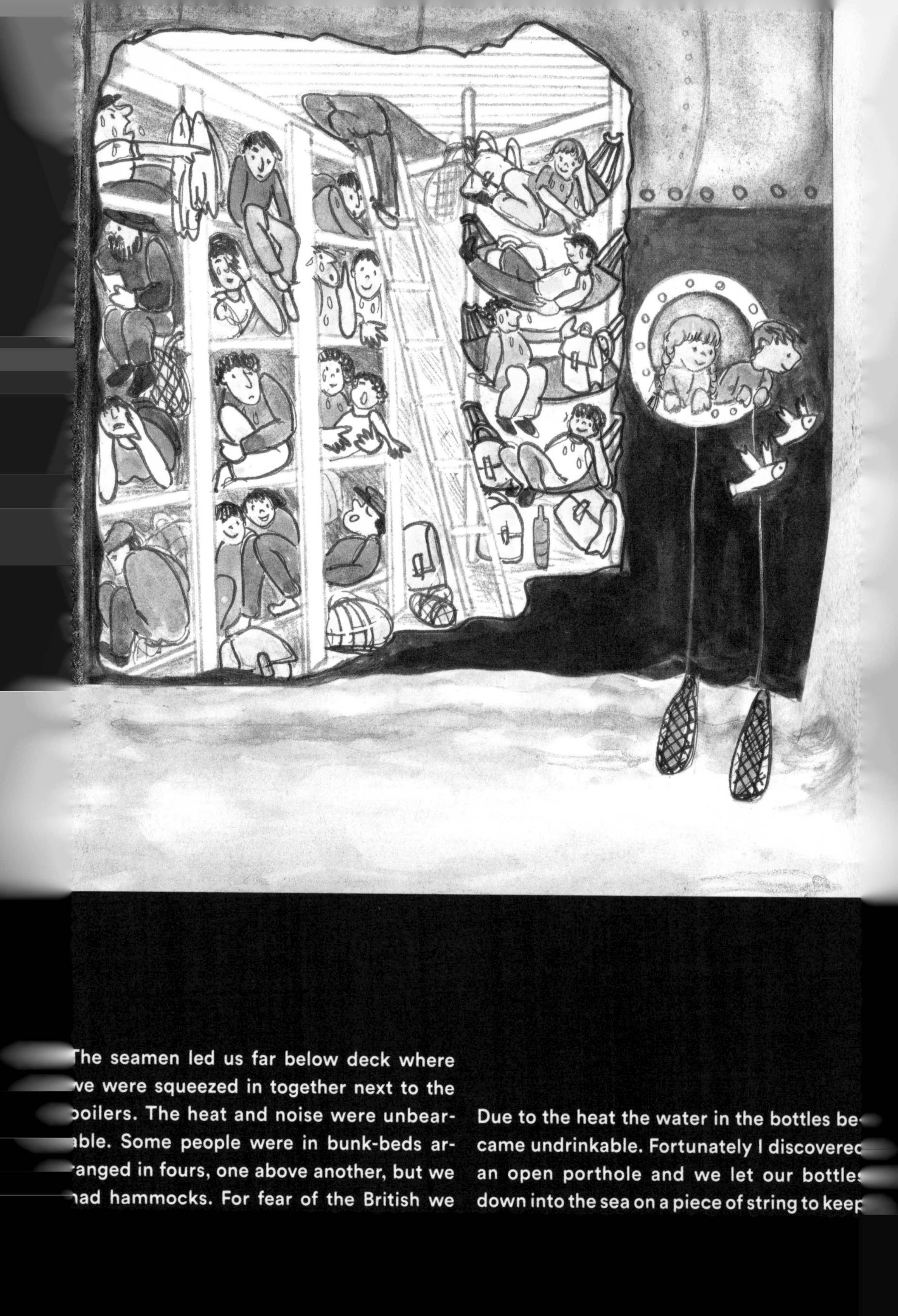

The seamen led us far below deck where we were squeezed in together next to the boilers. The heat and noise were unbearable. Some people were in bunk-beds arranged in fours, one above another, but we had hammocks. For fear of the British we

Due to the heat the water in the bottles became undrinkable. Fortunately I discovered an open porthole and we let our bottles down into the sea on a piece of string to keep

The following night the ship stealthily crept out of the harbour – but the British knew that there were 4,500 Jews on board. They followed us throughout our whole journey in a destroyer, that is a warship. Shortly before our arrival, they let us know by wireless that we should turn around and go back. "We don't want you in Palestine". Our captain answered: "We're returning to our homeland, to Israel!" The flag of Israel was hoisted and a banner with the new name of our ship was rolled out: 'EXODUS 947'. The British bellowed: "Turn around!" and we shouted back: "We're going home!" We tried to slip past them but soon six warships surrounded us as they were much faster. It was clear that they would try to board our ship so we got ready for the fight. We put on all the clothes we had, one layer on top of another, so as not to feel any blows, then we put up barricades and gathered all the potatoes and tins of food we had, ready to bombard the British. These were our only weapons; we didn't have either pistols or rifles. Everyone knew what they had to do: we were ready to put up a fight.

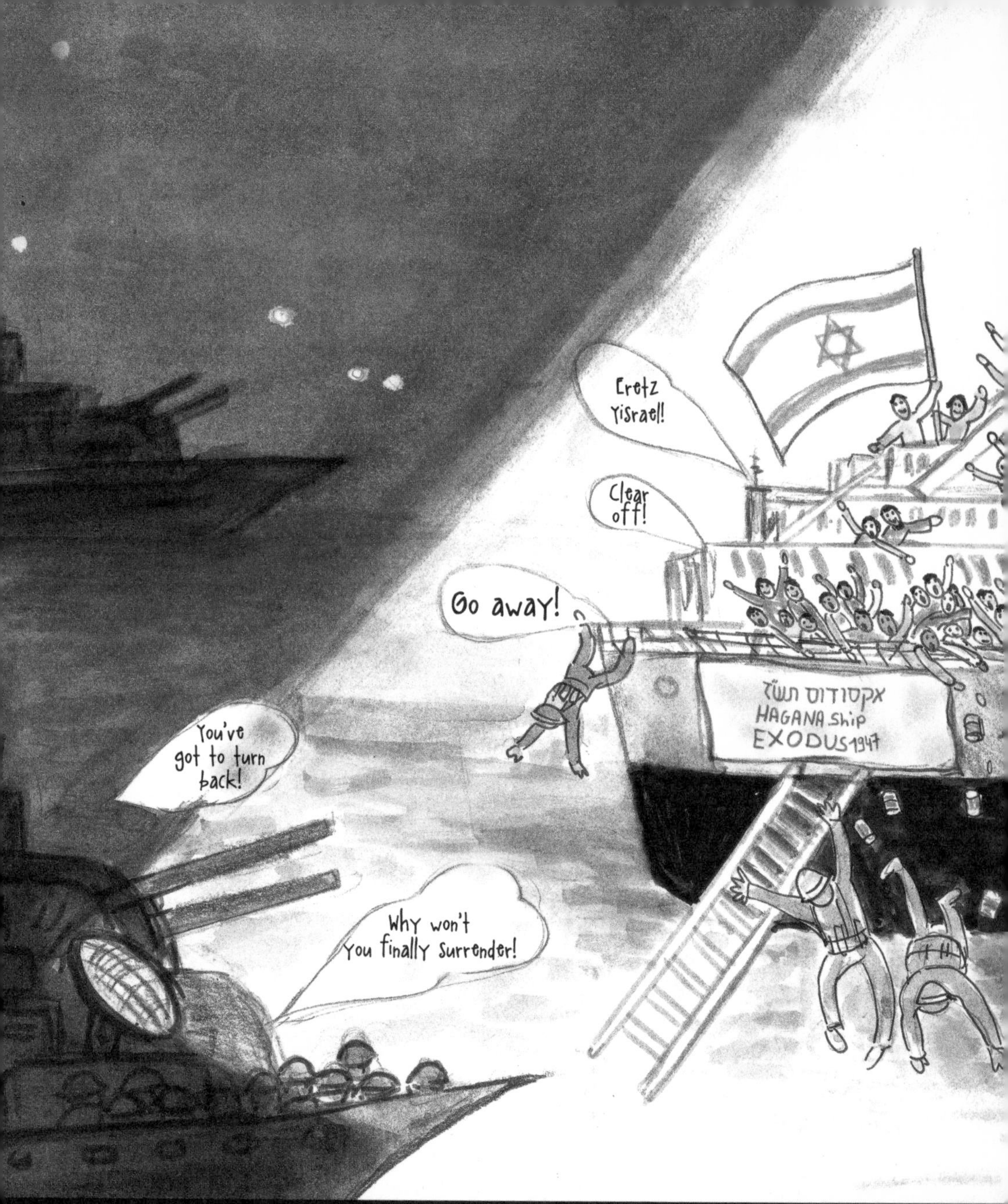
Eretz Yisrael!
Clear off!
Go away!
You've got to turn back!
Why won't You finally Surrender!
אקסודוס תשז
HAGANA ship
EXODUS 1947

n the middle of the night a siren suddenly went off and spotlights lit up the ship. The battle of the refugees on the Exodus against the British army had begun. Three war-ships drew up alongside and sprayed us with tear gas. Our eyes were burning terribly. The soldiers were wearing gas masks and helmets and tried to board the ship with adders and ropes. They were also carrying truncheons. The refugees fought back with

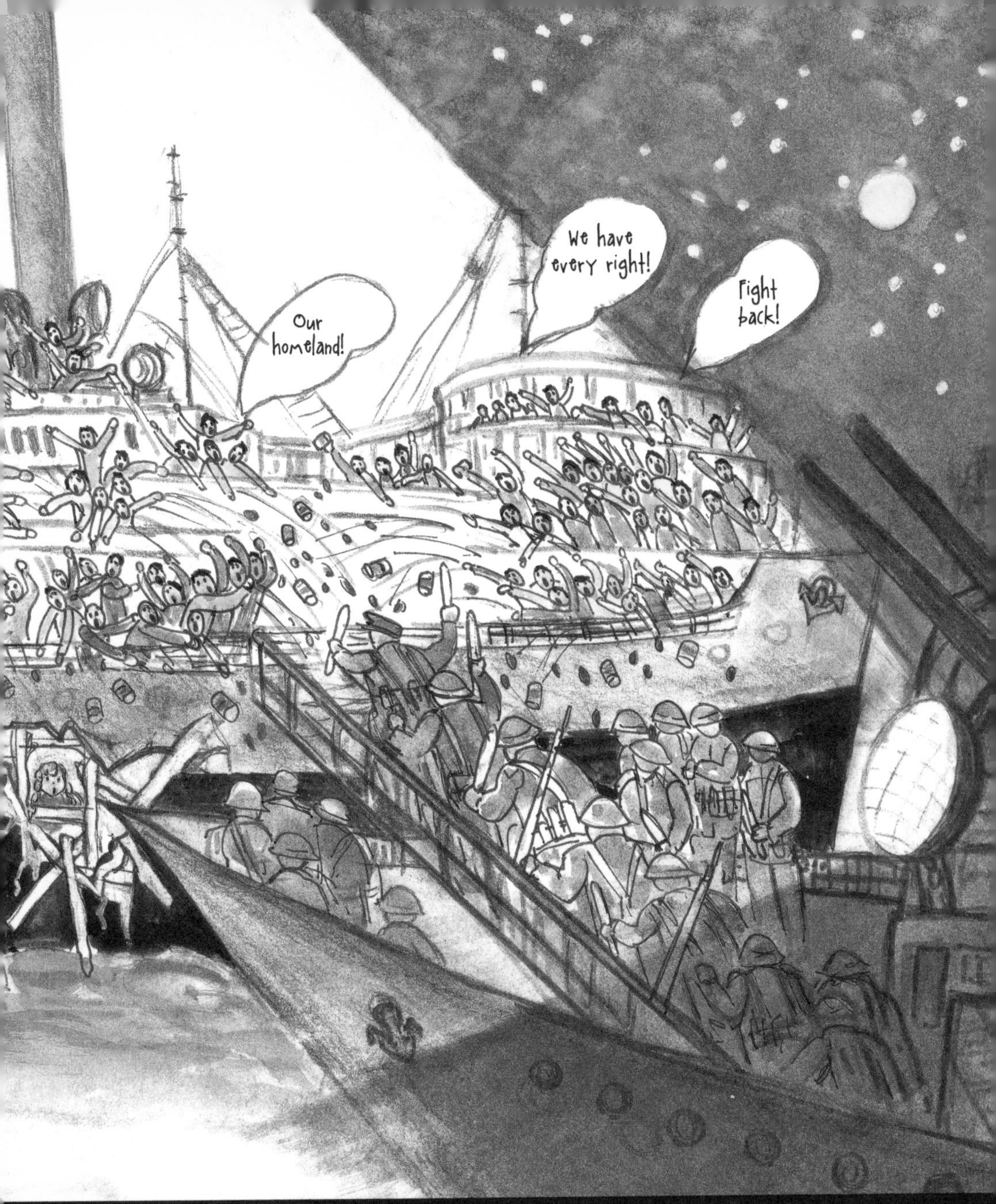
Our homeland!
We have every right!
Fight back!

tins of food and potatoes and pushed the ladders away so that the soldiers fell in the water.
When they saw that they weren't going to win so easily they turned their guns on us and opened fire. One child was killed. The captain of the Exodus ordered all children

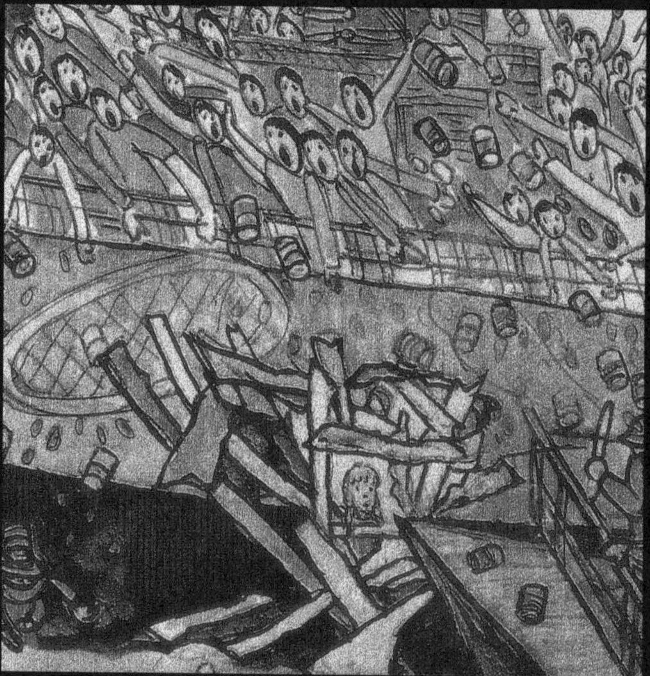

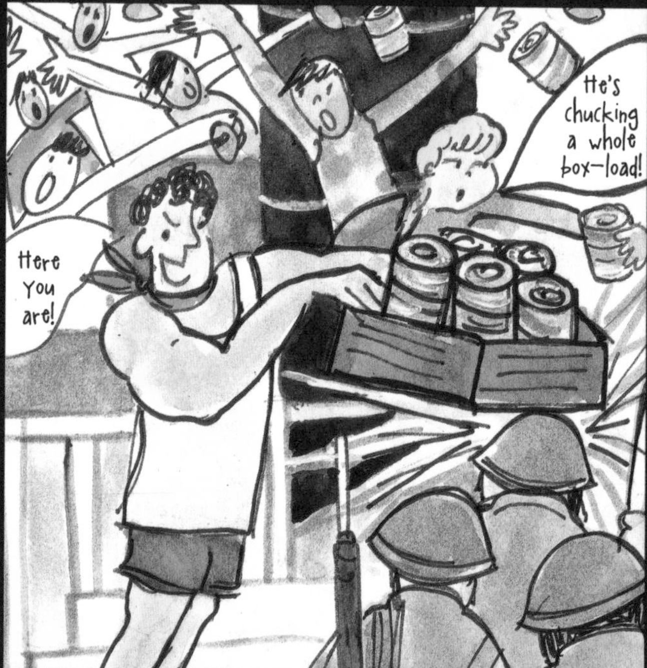
He's chucking a whole box-load!
Here You are!

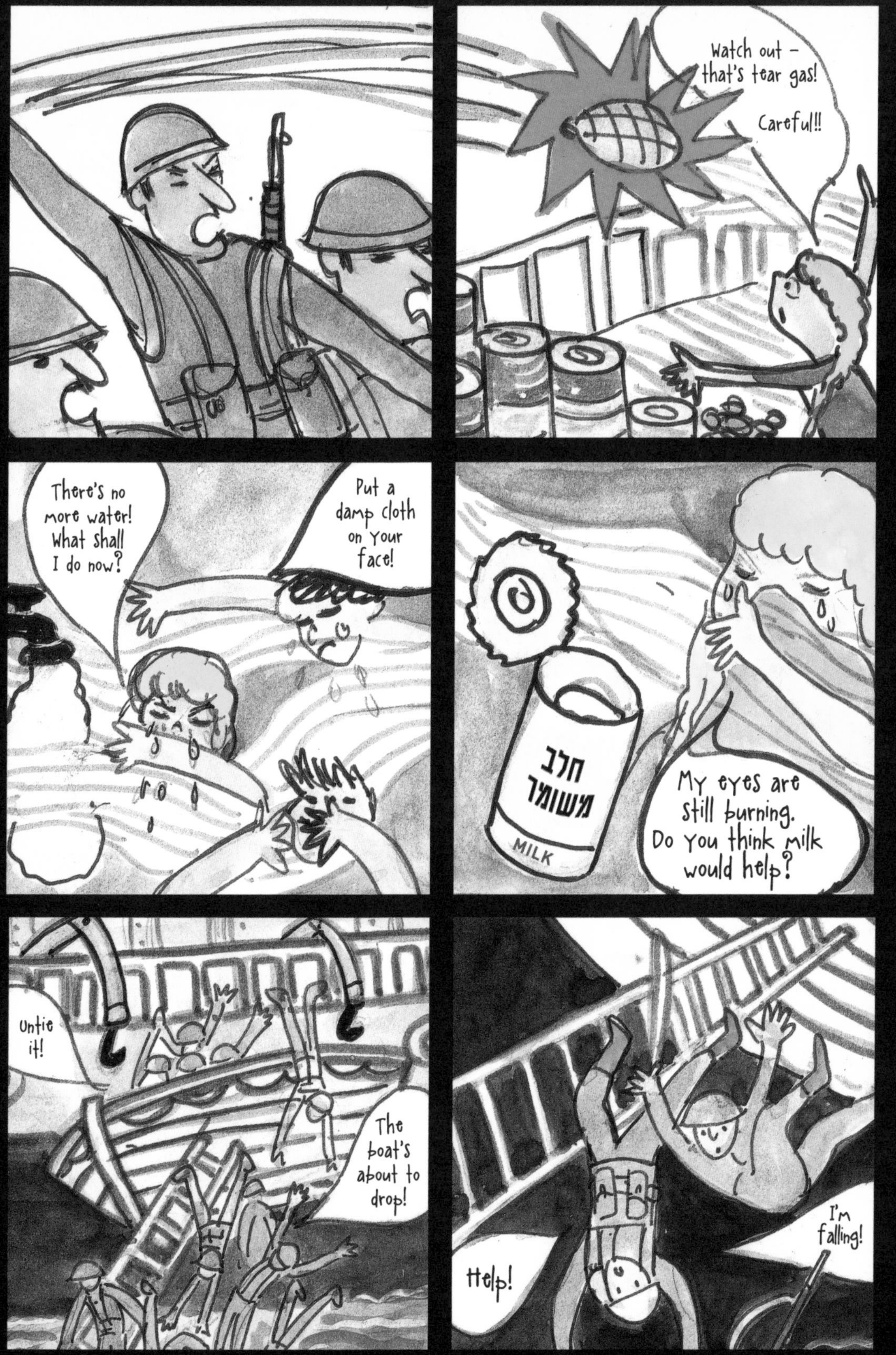
Watch out – that's tear gas!
Careful!!
There's no more water! What shall I do now?
Put a damp cloth on your face!
חלב משומר
MILK
My eyes are still burning. Do you think milk would help?
Untie it!
The boat's about to drop!
Help!
I'm falling!

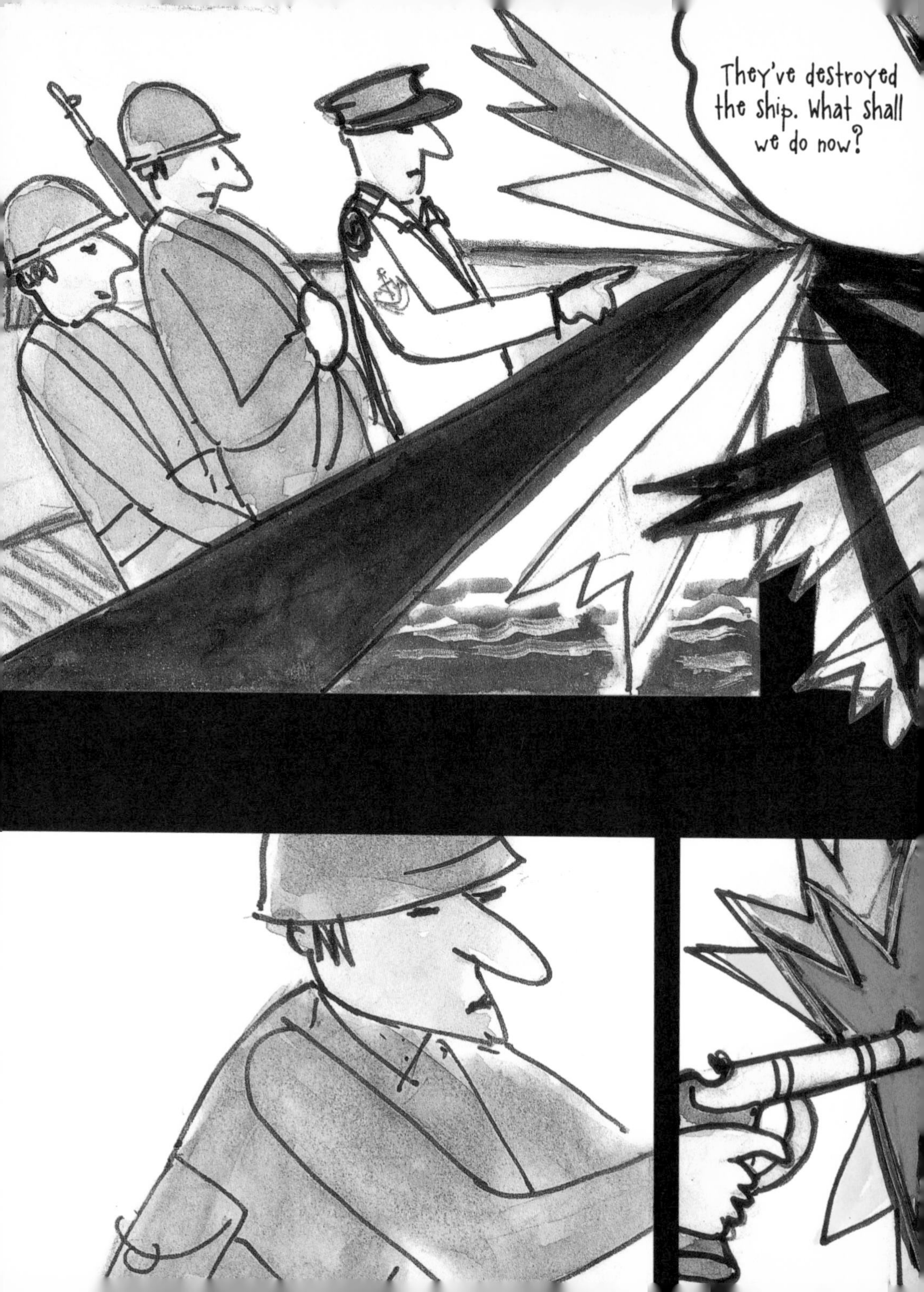
They've destroyed the ship. What shall we do now?

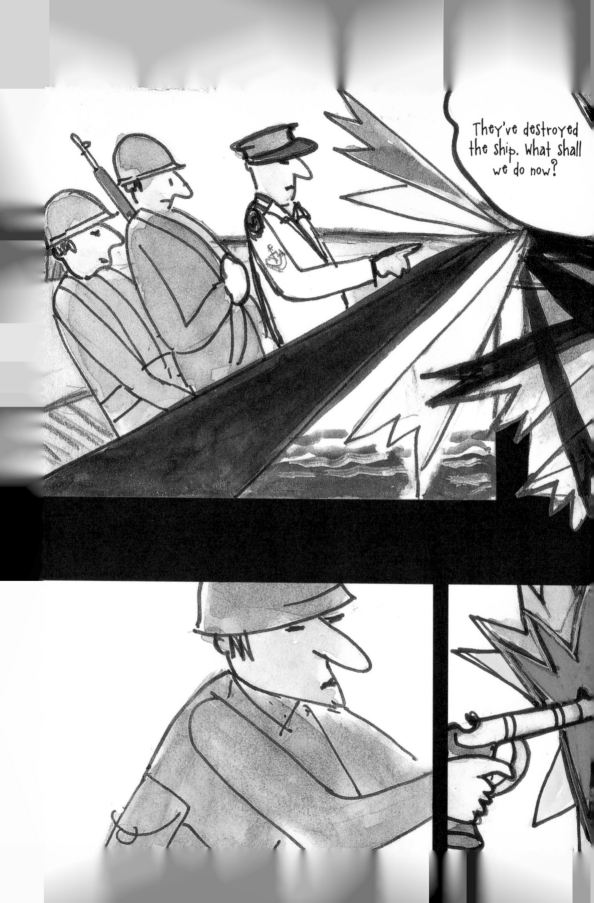

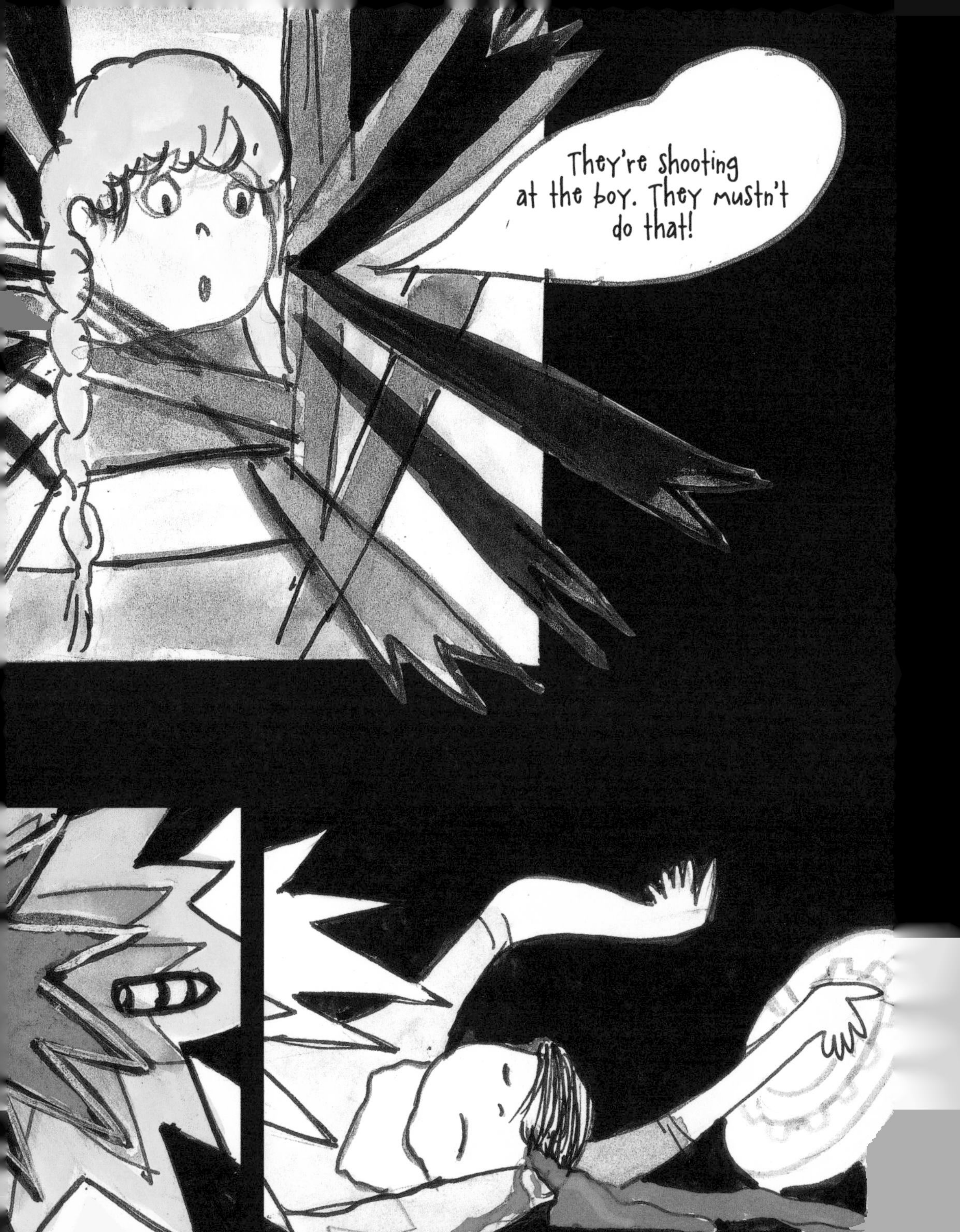
They're shooting at the boy. They mustn't do that!

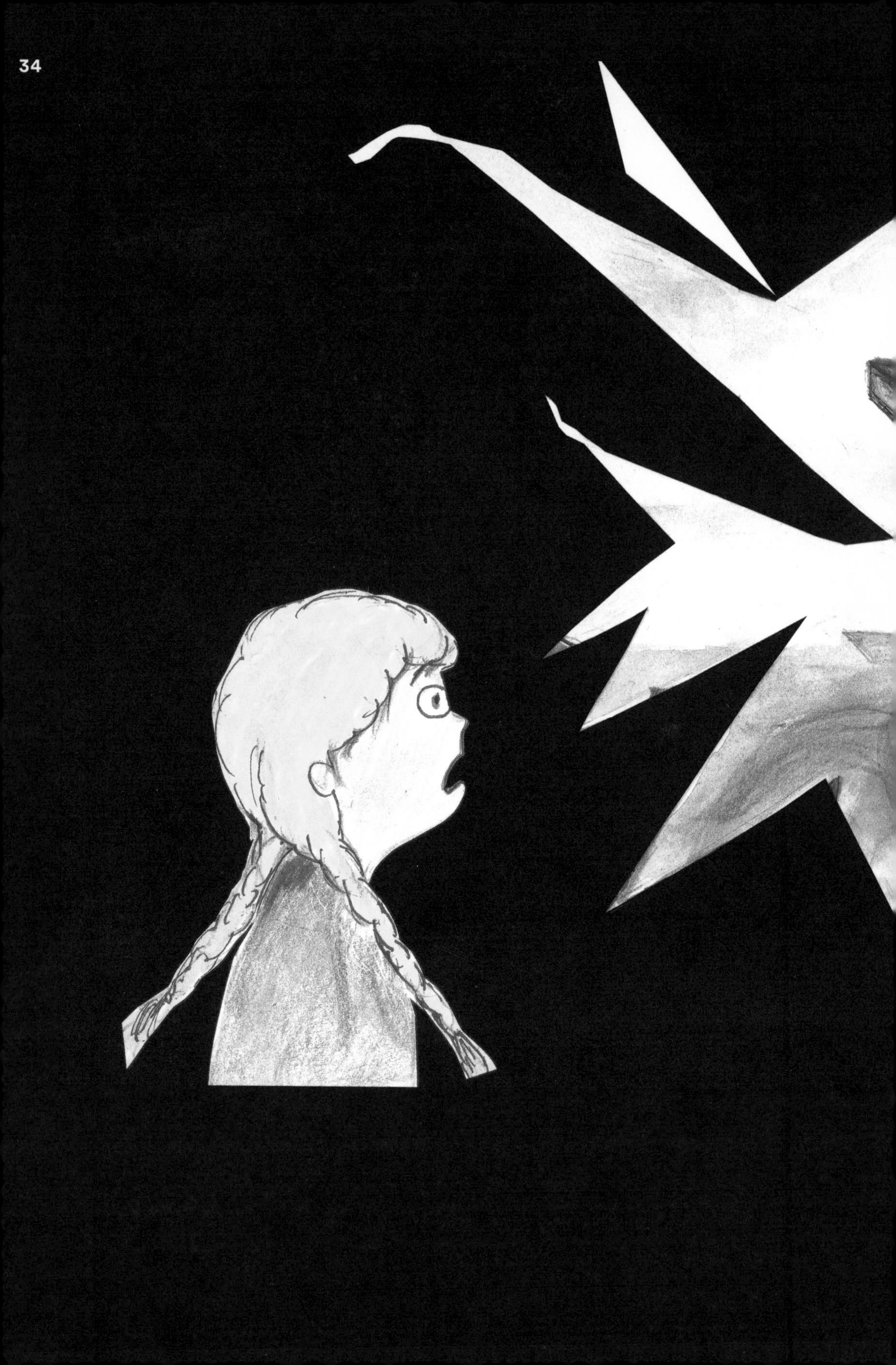

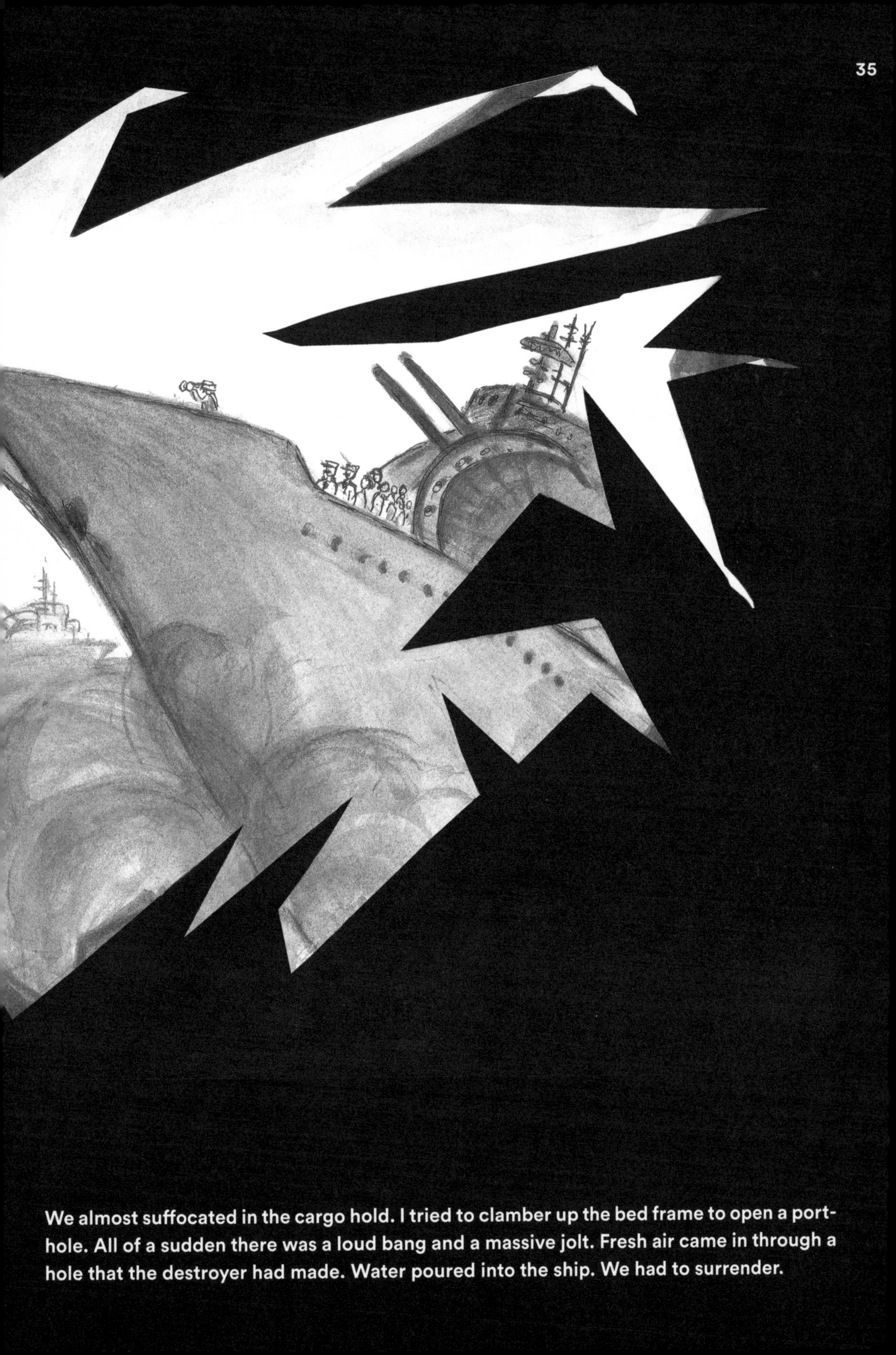

We almost suffocated in the cargo hold. I tried to clamber up the bed frame to open a port-hole. All of a sudden there was a loud bang and a massive jolt. Fresh air came in through a hole that the destroyer had made. Water poured into the ship. We had to surrender.

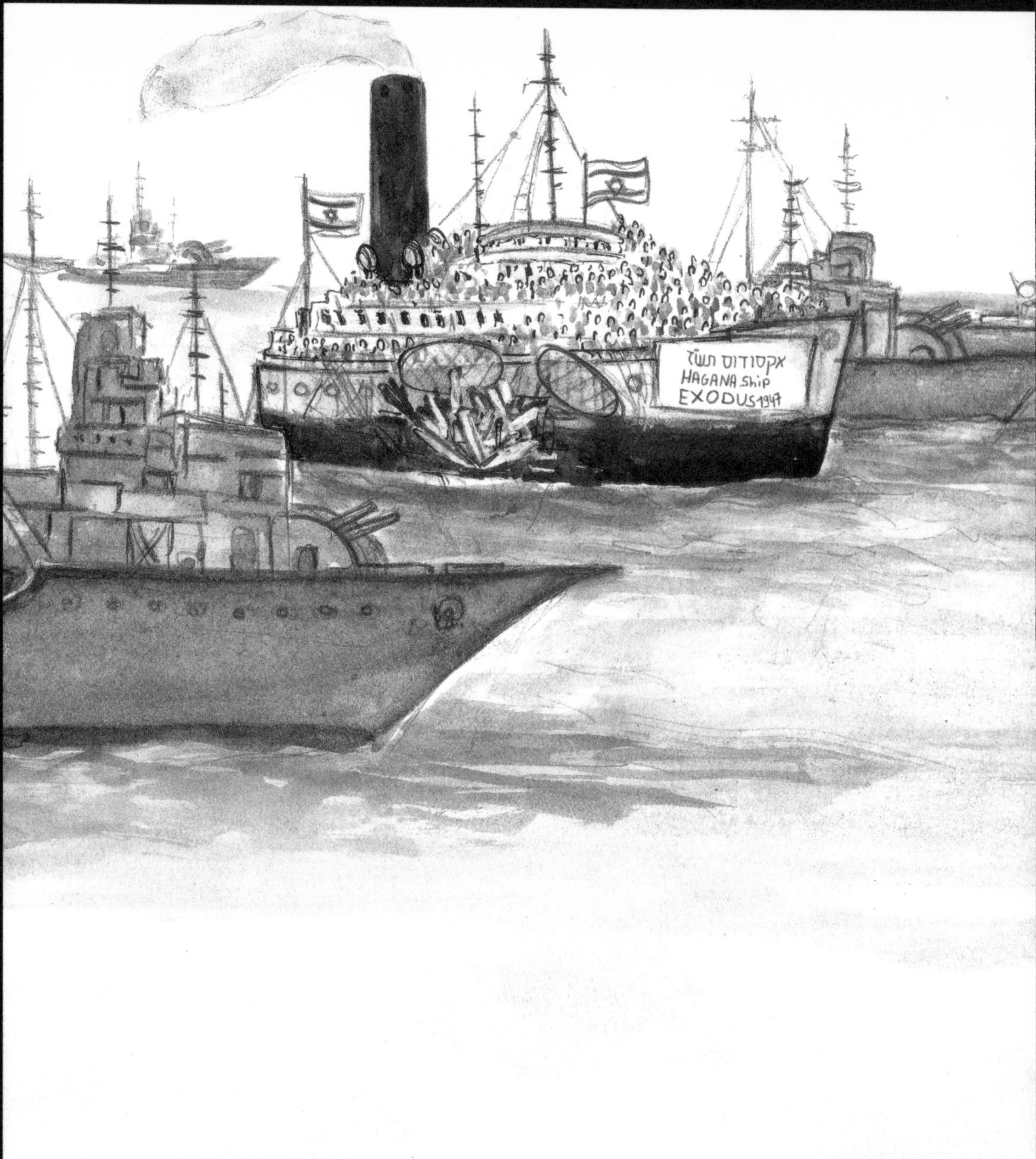
אקסודוס תשז
HAGANA ship
EXODUS 1947

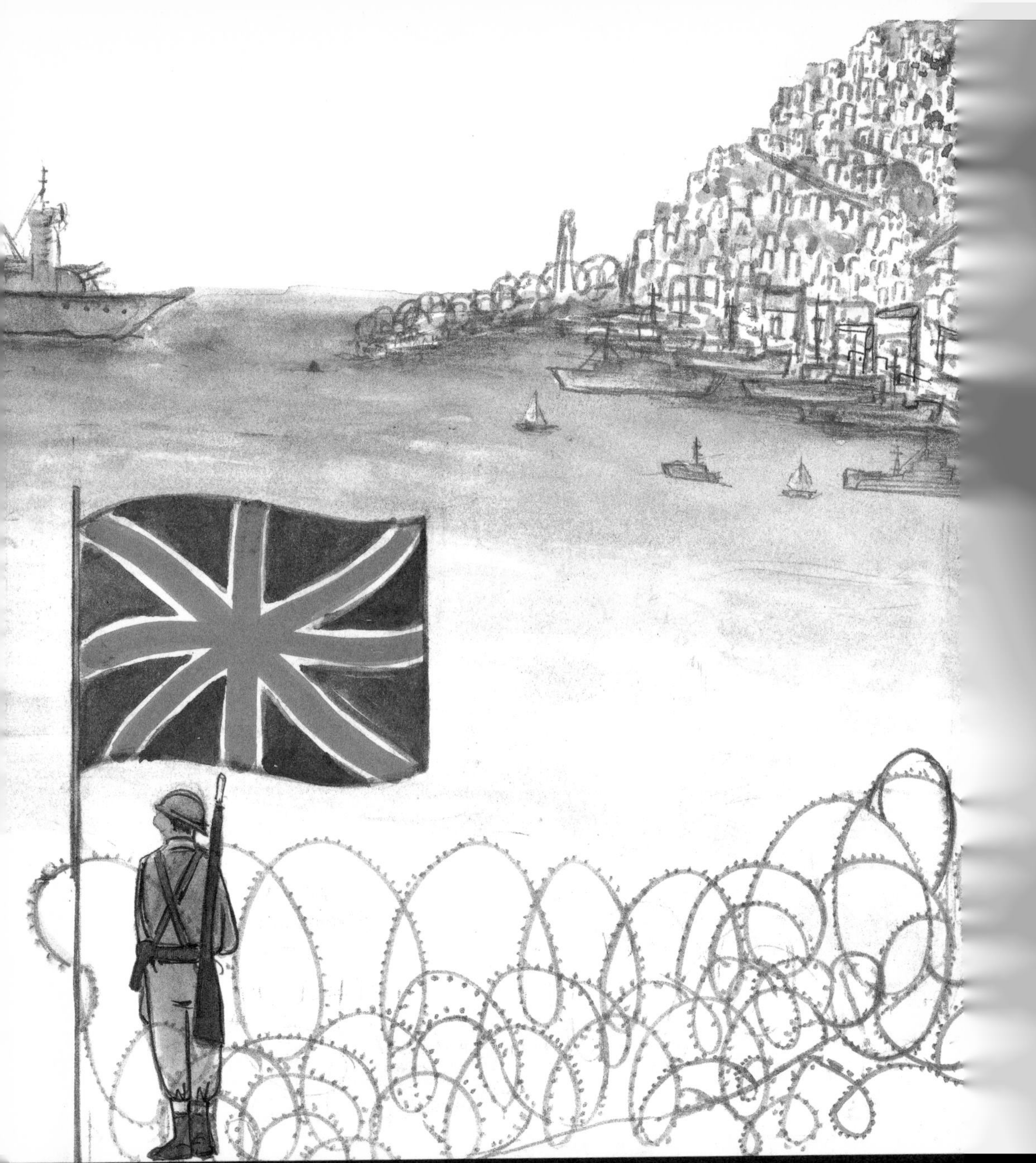

British soldiers seized our boat at dawn. They were wearing helmets and carrying guns, and had rubber truncheons and shields. The destroyers towed us away. In the afternoon we arrived at the port of Haifa – the beautiful city of Haifa. But we weren't allowed to go

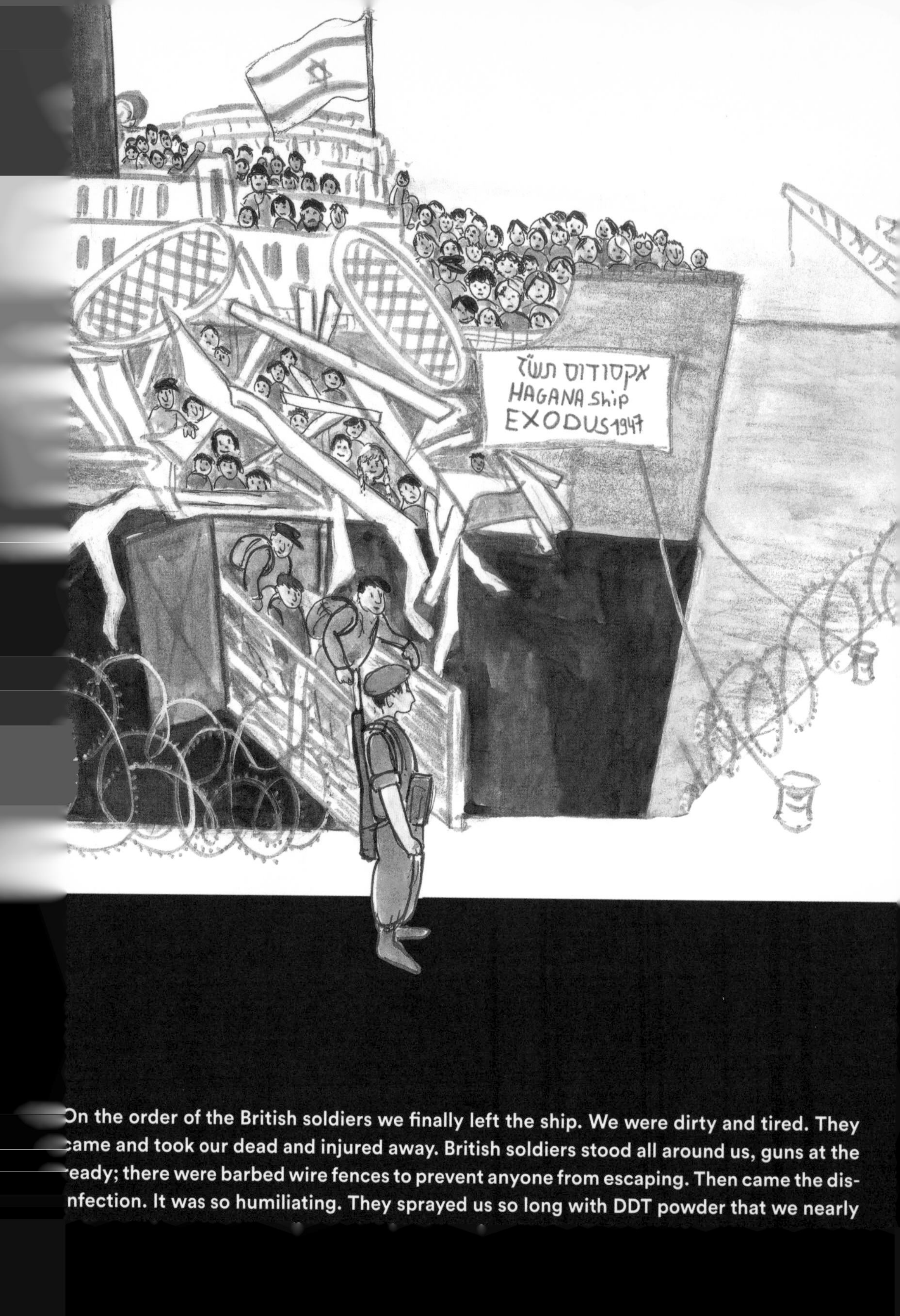
אקסודוס תש״ז
HAGANA Ship
EXODUS 1947

On the order of the British soldiers we finally left the ship. We were dirty and tired. They came and took our dead and injured away. British soldiers stood all around us, guns at the ready; there were barbed wire fences to prevent anyone from escaping. Then came the disinfection. It was so humiliating. They sprayed us so long with DDT powder that we nearly

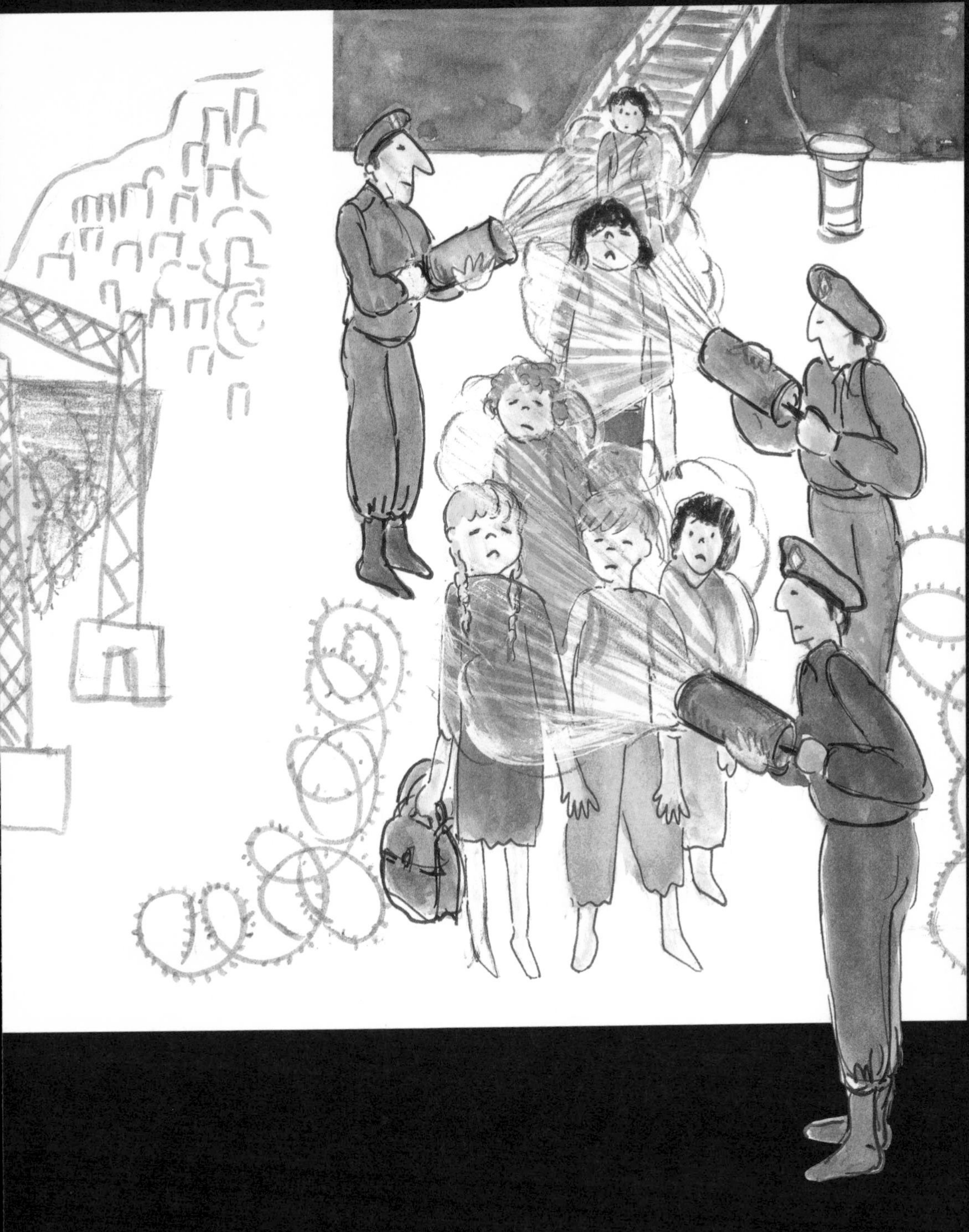

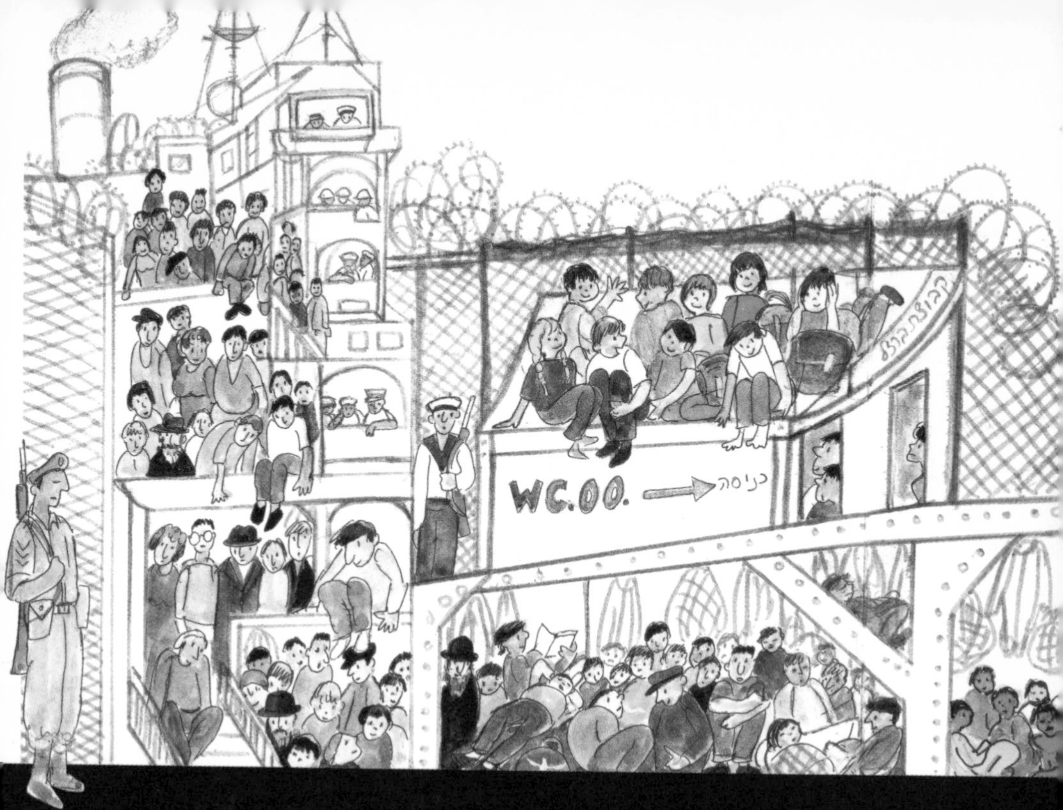
WC.00.
כניסה

We were divided up onto three big ships. They looked like huge floating prisons with high wire-mesh fences. My friends and I were the last to board. Our ship was called 'Empire Royal' and had previously been used to transport livestock. We were squeezed in tightly. Then we clambered up onto the roof above the lavatories and put up a tent over our heads.

We thought that we would be taken to the camp on Cyprus that was just a few days journey away. But the ships carried on sailing around on the open sea for three whole weeks. We saw nothing but the sky and the water until we finally reached the French coast and dropped anchor in the little harbour town of Port-de-Bouc.

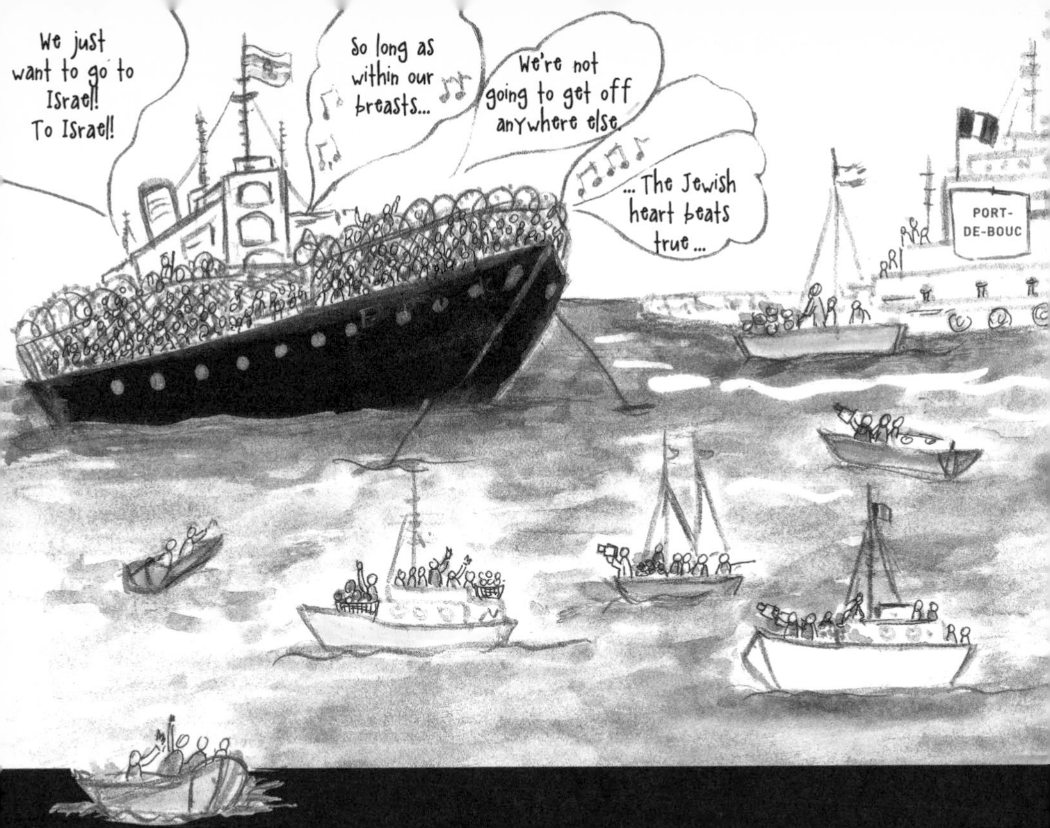
We just want to go to Israel! To Israel!
So long as within our breasts...
We're not going to get off anywhere else.
... The Jewish heart beats true ...
PORT-DE-BOUC

The British told us: "You're now back in France again where you set off on the Exodus. It's a lovely country – so you must leave the ships! The French will take you in." But we answered in unison: "We're not going to get off until we reach our homeland, Eretz Yisrael." The water around us us fruit, vegetables and even fresh bread. To thank each boat that drew alongside we sang our national anthem, the 'HaTikvah'. Every day the British tried to make us leave the ships. In the end they said: "If you don't want to get off, then we'll take you to Germany." And so the ships set off once again, heading out

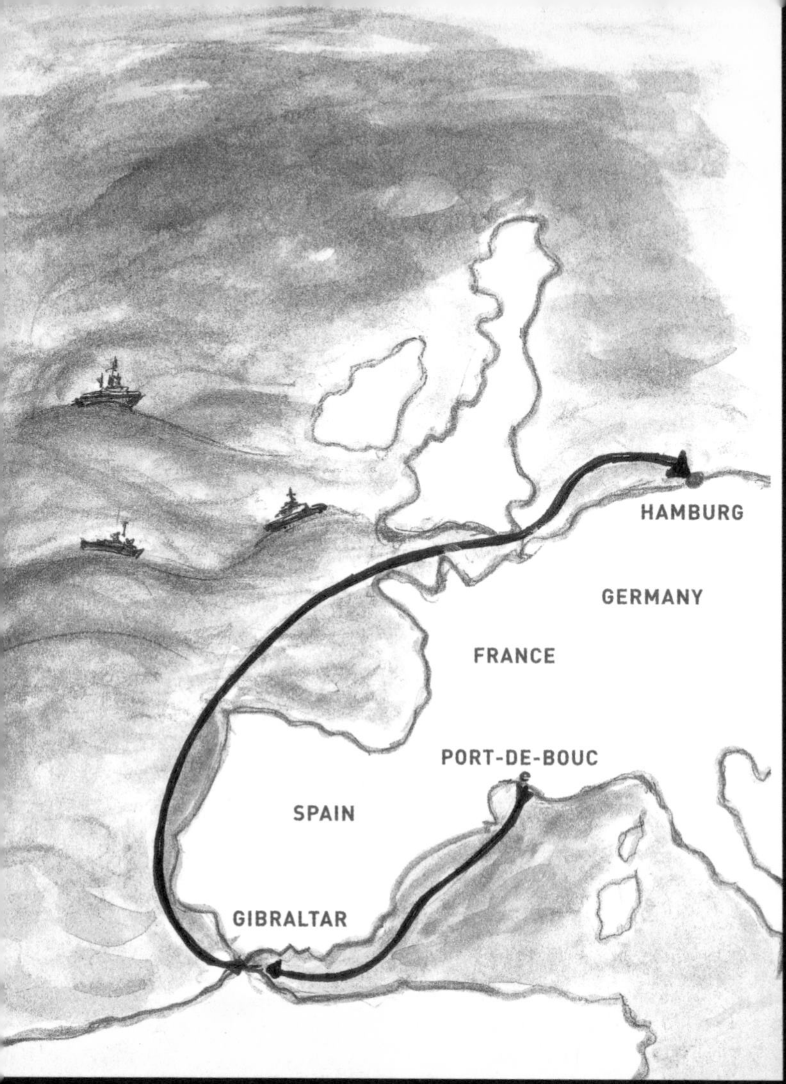
HAMBURG
GERMANY
FRANCE
PORT-DE-BOUC
SPAIN
GIBRALTAR

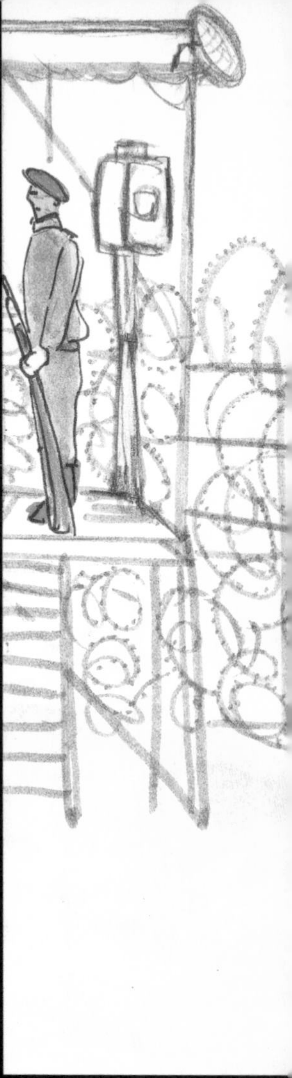

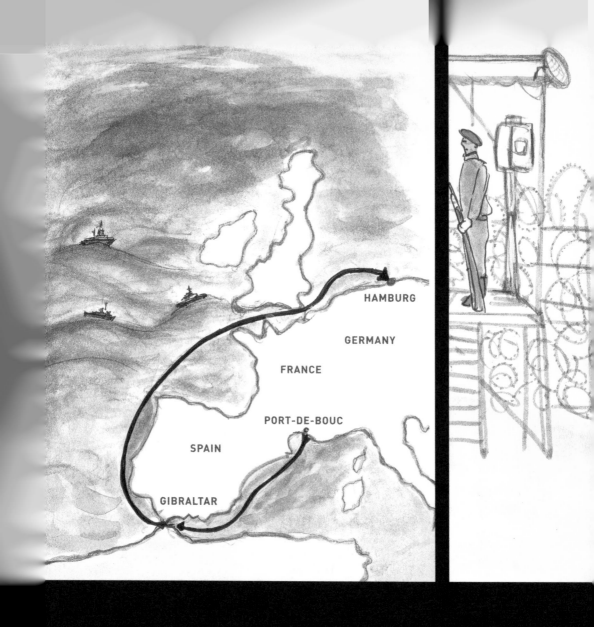

The ships sailed towards the ocean. Just sky and water once again. We passed through the Strait of Gibraltar and headed northwards up the Atlantic coast. The sea was menacing; huge waves rocked the ship from side to side and lots of people were seasick.

When we passed through the English Channel we could see houses, cars and people on the shore. We finally reached Hamburg

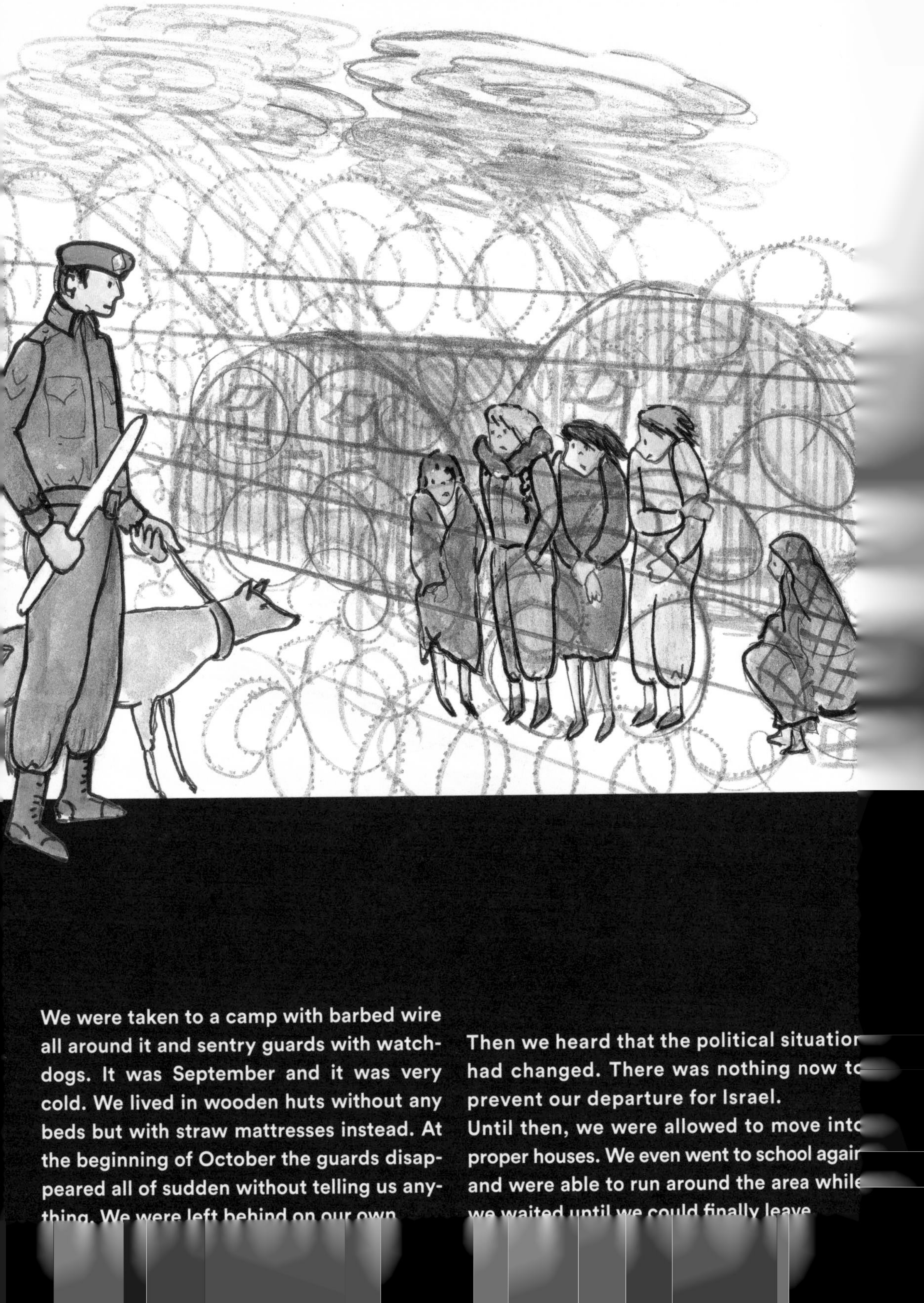

We were taken to a camp with barbed wire all around it and sentry guards with watch-dogs. It was September and it was very cold. We lived in wooden huts without any beds but with straw mattresses instead. At the beginning of October the guards disappeared all of sudden without telling us anything. We were left behind on our own.

Then we heard that the political situation had changed. There was nothing now to prevent our departure for Israel.
Until then, we were allowed to move into proper houses. We even went to school again and were able to run around the area while we waited until we could finally leave.

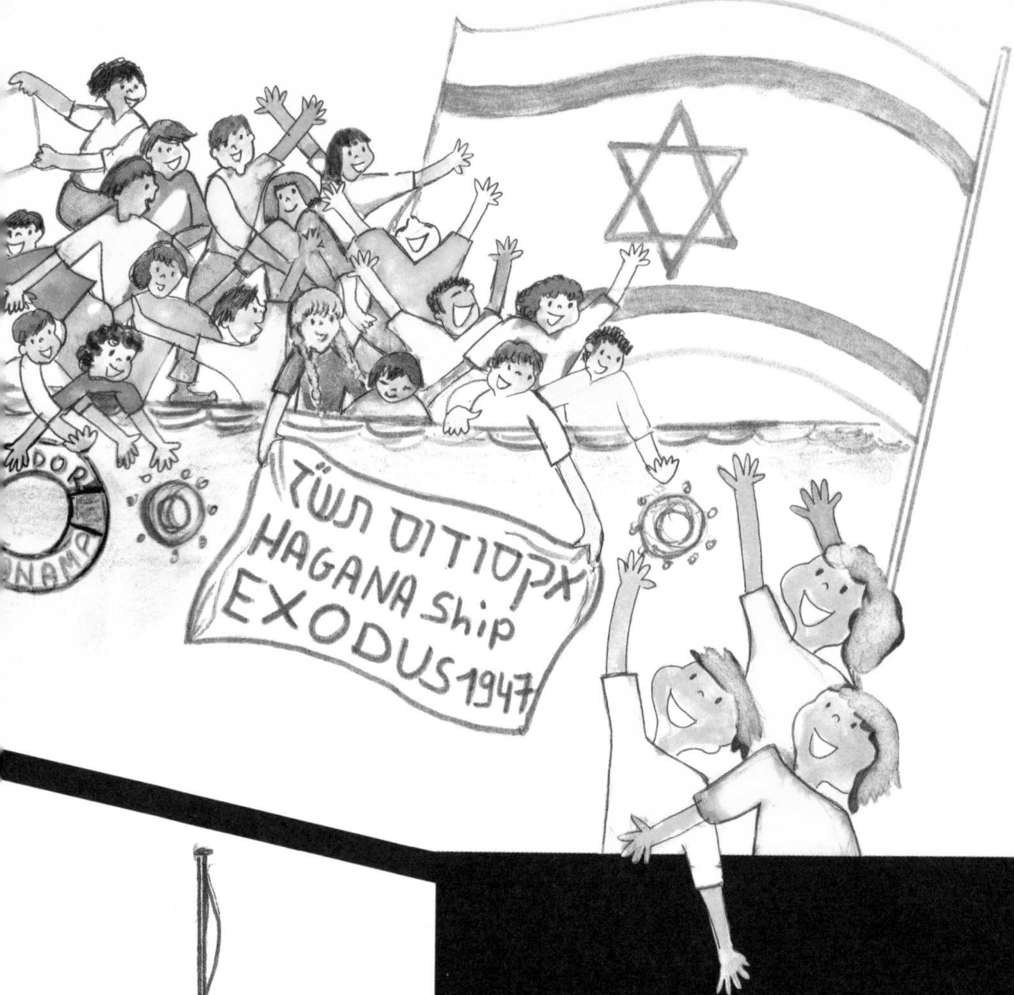
אקסודוס תש״ז
HAGANA Ship
EXODUS 1947

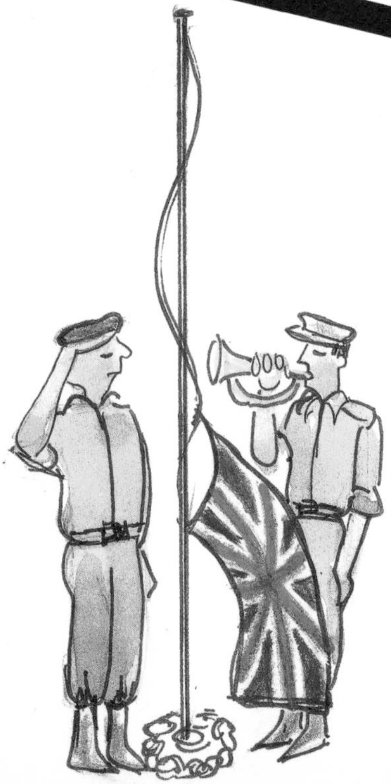

With the coming of spring things started moving. This time we travelled on a big white ship called the 'Andorra Panama'. We reached Israel in May 1948 on the day that the last British soldiers left the country. We even saw them lowering the flag opposite the wreck of the Exodus, on the very same shore where we had been forced into the cages. British rule had come to an end!

We were taken to the kibbutz 'Sdot Yam' – that means 'fields by the sea'. We felt safe there straight away and our kibbutz became a real home.

That first evening I went to the beach. The sun was setting like a red fireball dipping into the sea. A slight breeze was blowing

At long last I finally had the feeling that had come home.

I sat down on the warm sand.

I was happy.

But …

I also felt like crying.

How I wished Mummy and Daddy were

IMPRINT

Published by
Hirmer Publishers
Bayerstrasse 57–59
80335 Munich
Germany

© 2020 Hirmer Publishers
Title of the Hebrew 1st edition: TIKA'S JOURNEY
© 2008 Schocken Publishing House Ltd.,
Tel Aviv, Israel
Text and Illustration:
© Esther Shakine

www.hirmerpublishers.com

TRANSLATION
Christopher Wynne, Bad Toelz

COPY-EDITING / PROOFREADING
Jane Michael, Munich

PROJECT MANAGEMENT
Gabriele Ebbecke, Munich

DESIGN / TYPESETTING
Marion Blomeyer, Munich

PRE-PRESS / REPRO
Reproline mediateam GmbH, Munich

PRINTING / BINDING
Westermann Druck Zwickau GmbH

Bibliographic information published by the Deutsche
Nationalbibliothek
The Deutsche Nationalbibliothek lists this publication
in the Deutsche Nationalbibliografie; detailed bibliographic data are available on the Internet at http://
dnb.dnb.de.

ISBN 978-3-7774-3553-4

Printed in Germany